GW01457931

Yäqteenya

THE OLD WORLD

Yassar Bahjatt
@YBahjatt

يتخيلون
The League of Arabic SciFiers

Sales@Yatakhayaloon.com
Info@Yatakhayaloon.com
ISBN: 9948180976
ISBN-13: 978-9948-18-097-5

Acknowledgment

I would like to thank Dr. Arlan Andrews, Sr., who put me on the spot during his session in GCF2012, forcing me to think seriously about the Arabian Science Fiction industry and how to help in its creation, as well as his continuous support. I also thank Arthur Zards, who pushed me to pitch my sci-fi impact concept to TED, giving me a much-needed boost to move forward with Yatakhayaloon. Last but not least, I would like to thank TED's Open Translation Project for the translation experience I had built through the program, as it was the first platform where I published my translation work. This experience was essential for me to now be able to author this novel.

The Beginning

ياسر بهجت Yasser Bahjatt

Wednesday the eleventh of Thul Qidah[1] of the 584th year since the fall of Granada (FG)

I have to write this down before it all disappears. I do not have much time to explain who I am or how I am sending these words to you. All you need to know for now is that I am a historian. I study history, specializing in the sub-discipline of causal history, where we study history as a chain of successive events, each one causing a change in historical course, leading us to the next event. I started this particular study when I discovered an Andalucían document that completely changed my understanding of history. I will explain more when I have time, but for now, I need to transmit to you the actual text of these historical documents that I found during my research that spanned two decades and several continents. I will try to transmit the contents of the documents, as each of them is very important. For that reason, I will transmit each document in its entirety before I move on to the next. There is no specified order to these documents. I will order them according to my view of their importance to help you build a clear and complete image. Even though most of what you will receive is the text from these

---

[1] The Arabian twelve lunar months are Rabee the former, Rabee the latter, Jumad the former, Jumad the latter, Rajab, Shaban, Ramadan, Shawal, Thul Qidah, Thul Hijjah, Moharram, and Safar.

5

documents in front of me, I will comment on portions and fill in the gaps with what I know. If a document was damaged in that part, I will inform you to maintain the scientific integrity of my work, on which I spent a lifetime to uncover those facts. I am also working hard on preparing a data storage mechanism that can hold all the facts and signs of our history and culture to help you better understand these documents and their depth.

One of these documents is the memoirs of Al-Baz Al-Monqad[1] (I will be attaching the literal translation of most names or provide some cultural context so you might better understand them in the context of these notes). Despite the importance of these memoirs, they are not sorted in chronological order, as it seems that Al-Baz did not write his memoirs day after day, rather he wrote them when his memories were revived during more important events, taking him back to other events that he thought were related to them. That is what makes it a central document to this historical study, as it is the oldest known complete causal history document.

---

[1] Al-Baz Al-Monqad—Translation: Striking Eagle.

(1)

Okeanós

Yasser Bahjatt ياسر بهجت

The final days of Rabee the latter 291 FG

Three days have passed since I escaped my captors. I think they are still looking for me to question me so that they can go to my country and finish what they started three centuries ago: eliminate Islam and its followers. I pray to Allah to spare me such an ordeal, to not put me in that position, and to not make me the cause of unveiling the secret of my country after he had hidden it from them. I try to hide and sleep during the day and move at night, which makes it harder for them to track me down. Of course, this makes my own mission much more difficult. I need to find what remains of my shipwreck to gather my tools and books that I will need to continue my expedition and complete my mission.

I don't know exactly how much time has passed since my shipwreck, but Rabee the latter's crescent was about to disappear. The last thing I remember was the storm that night, the night[1] of Sunday, the twenty-third of Rabee the latter. The Okeanós's waves were tossing the ship around like a kid's toy passed between a bunch of guys to prevent its owner from getting to it. The sky was filled with black clouds, and the Okeanós was lit up by the lightning. The air

---

[1] In Arabian culture, night comes before day, so the night of Sunday (or Saturday Night) is the night before Sunday.

rumbled with the crashing sounds of thunderclaps. I noticed that the time between the lightning and sounds of thunder was decreasing, thereby assuring us that no matter how hard we tried, we would not escape this storm, and that all our efforts to avoid its center had failed. Everyone was concentrating all their efforts on getting through the storm with minimal losses, but the captain said that this storm was the worst he had ever experienced, as he had never crossed the Okeanós before. The ship's deck was in complete chaos as they tried to lower the sail that had suddenly wrapped itself around the mast! The sky lit up at the same moment we heard the thunder, so we had reached the eye of the storm. The thunder was so strong that it echoed across the ship, especially off the ship's starboard side, where the lightning had struck. I guess the human brain handles time differently during a crisis, as I could almost swear that time had halted for a moment after the flash of lightning before the ship's side exploded in a flash much brighter than the lightning itself. Our world was in total disarray. Most of the sailors were busy on the ship's deck, as losing control over the sail meant our assured destruction. The continued flow of water meant we would sink. The captain surprised me when he held me by the shoulder and pulled me, ordering me to the ship's hull to help stop the water intake. When I went down below, I found the ship filled with two opposites that rarely coexist: water *filled the ship, while fire also ravaged across it. We tried to control the water by fixing the sides of the ship from within, but to no avail. The opening that the lightning had caused was two men high, and at least ten arms across. I remember holding a plank of wood, trying to hold it in place, as one of the sailors hammered it. The sky lit up again and I saw a giant wave coming toward us. I held onto the side of the ship as hard as I could, and closed my eyes, waiting for the moment the cold sea water would impact my body. Time passed so slowly. I remembered all the events that led me to this moment, the events that started with disorder that blanketed Yaqteenya.*

How did it all start? How did it tear us apart? How it shook people's beliefs. I remembered my mother's fear when she realized what I was planning to do, to find out the truth and stop this madness; how I escaped my imprisonment that my father had put me in to stop me from breaking the first law of Yaqteenya, which forbade me from crossing the Okeanós; how I got to this ship and how I was able to avoid the soldiers to speed east across the Okeanós.

All of those memories crashed in my head like the waves were crashing in the sea in front of me then, and with that thought, I remembered the wave that seemed to have taken a lifetime to reach me. I opened my eyes in the same moment its freezing water covered me. I tried to hold onto anything, but the sea pulled me out and threw me into its crashing waves. I wrestled the Okeanós to prevent it from swallowing

11

me… and then the world went dark.

◦❖❖❖❖❖❖❖❖◦

All my senses came alive at once. I was laying on my face on a beach where the sun had fired up its sand to temperatures that I had never experienced. I have no idea how much time had passed while I was in that position. My entire body ached, and my back was burned by the sun and salt. Waves were slamming my feet and I was very thirsty. I felt footsteps in the water closing in on me. Every cell in my body came to life. I did not move, hoping that I was wrong, or that he would just move away from me, but if the rumors about this land were true, then there was no escape from its people, and they would not leave me alone. The steps stopped and I felt the tip of a sword poking my back. At that moment, all of my energy returned and I remembered everything I had learned in the art of fighting, most importantly the element of surprise. I moved my right leg, swiftly placing my right foot behind my assailant's leg, then pulling hard, throwing him off balance as he fell on his back while pulling his sword away from my back. I twisted my body around my waist; as my left foot kicked the sword out of his hand, throwing it away as I disarmed him, I fell on my back and felt an enormous amount of pain when it touched the hot sand that was wet, dampened with sea water because of its burns. I ignored the pain, though, as I needed to stand up before my adversary did. I pushed my body upward to stand up and look directly into my adversary's astonished eyes. I quickly ran directly toward him, knocking him unconscious with a swift kick to the head.

At that moment, I noticed the shadows around me. I turned to find that I was surrounded by eight warriors, each waving his sword at me. I took a fighting stance. While every bit of my body waited for the first move toward me, a strong, husky voice echoed from behind the warriors. "STOP!"

I turned to the source of the voice and froze for a second, as I saw a giant who was four arms tall, and had dark black skin, as black as a moonless night. He must be a marid[1], I thought. The thought did not have time to settle in my head, though, as I felt extreme pain at the back of my head, right before the world went dark again.

◦❖❖❖❖❖❖❖◦

I woke up from my slumber at the sound of the call to prayer, and for the second time, I found myself laying without any sense of time. I was laying on a wooden table in a cell with a window covered with iron bars, and on the facing side, the iron bars extended from the ceiling to the floor. In its center was a door. The cell seemed to be on one side of a wide yard. I could clearly see several wooden boxes piled

---

[1] Marid is a powerful class of Jinn.

against the wall facing my cell. I was almost certain that they were from my ship. I could hear the soft sound of waves. We must have been near a beach. I grabbed onto the bars of the window to pull myself up, hoping to figure out where I was or at least figure out my bearings and the direction of the Qiblah[1]. I saw the sun setting in the Okeanós directly facing my window. I sat on the floor as I looked around. There were stone walls, with words and symbols engraved in them. My cell had a high ceiling. In one corner, there was a pitcher, and in the center was a plate with some scattered food. I picked up the pitcher and smelled it to verify what was in it and then took a sip because I was extremely thirsty. I poured some of it on my hands and performed Wudu[2]. I stood with my back to the window and started my prayer. I had this strange feeling that I cannot really explain, but I will try. I felt that I was semi-nude. My shirt was torn, but I was not naked. No, the reason for that strange feeling was that, for the first time in my life, I was praying without gripping my sword's hilt in my right hand, as it was hanging off the left side of my waist. I also was not holding my dagger's hilt in my left hand, as it was hanging on my right shoulder. Had they disarmed me? Or had I lost them in the Okeanós, as its waves toyed with me? I do not remember. I realized that I had lost my focus from

---

[1] Qiblah is the direction of Makkah, as Muslims have to pray facing it.

[2] Wudu is sometimes translated as ablution.

14

my prayer. I tried to focus again by pushing my
brain away from thinking of the situation I was in,
while focusing on the verses I was reading, but it
seemed that fate did not want me to focus on my
prayers in that place and time, as my senses
awakened while I was on the floor. I heard footsteps
approaching my cell. My reaction was spontaneous; I
squeezed my left grip (which was on my right
shoulder) in an involuntary movement, expecting to
squeeze my daggers hilt in anticipation of pulling it,
if the situation so demanded. I felt the pain of my
nails digging into my hand as it looked for the
dagger. I struggled to calm myself while I listened.
They were the steps of two men; one of them, it
seemed, was of a moderate height and body mass,
whereas the other was a giant. I could almost swear
he was that same marid that I saw at the beach. I
listened harder, trying to make out what they were
saying. At the start, their voices were very soft, so I
could not make out any words, but as they came
closer, I recognized one of their husky voices. It was
the marid. "But who is this man?" the marid asked.

"We do not know yet, but I have never seen a
shipwreck like this before."

"How come? It looks to me like any other boxes
thrown off a wrecked ship," said the marid.

"They are, but its contents are strange. It has
books written in Arabic by authors I have never heard
of before." His words stopped as his steps changed,
and I heard a dim sound, as if he was looking

through a bag that he was carrying. Then he added, "We also found these amongst the wreck."

"Whoever drew these must be very talented. Who are they? And what is this strange outfit? Have you ever seen anyone put such feathers in their turbans?" asked the marid in astonishment.

"The details and accuracy of this drawing could not have been made by a human." It seemed that they were talking about some of the shadows that they had found amongst my stuff. Strange! Had they never seen them before?! I had sat for my first tashahod[1] to find their legs moving in front of my cell and the marid standing exactly in front of me. I stood up. I was now facing them. I raised my eyes to inspect them, then my eyes met the marid's. I did not break my eye contact. I knelt down as they stopped talking. I completed my prayers, and when I was done, my eyes met with the marid's again and this time, I maintained the contact. I stood without moving my eyes away, trying to show that I was not afraid of him, and that I was his match.

"Who are you? And why did you attack my men?" asked the marid in a husky and clearly angry tone.

I did not care much for what he asked, but I needed to understand my situation. "How are you talking Arabic? And why did you call for prayers?"

---

[1] Tashahod is a step during the ritual of Islamic prayer where the worshiper is sitting on the ground.

"Strange! Had you not just performed your prayers? So why, then, do you ask about its call? What are those tools in your wreckage? And where are you from?" asked the marid. It's what I expected. He didn't even attempt to hide his interest in my country. I wouldn't tell him anything, though, as I did not want to be the cause for the destruction of Yaqteenya.

"I will not answer any of your questions until you answer me first. Who are you? How do you speak Arabic? Am I in Al-Andalus?" I had to know how they were able to retain their knowledge of Arabic and of Islamic rituals after they had eliminated the Arabs and Muslims from Al-Andalus!

"Al-Andalus! Al-Andalus fell almost three centuries ago," his assistant said, mockingly. The marid shot him an angry look that silenced him and forced him to retreat to the back wall and inspect my ship's wreckage.

The marid returned his look. "You are in Morocco, south of what was once called Al-Andalus. I am Agha Antarah, the head of the Ottoman army in this country, and that is Kahyabak Hamzah. Do you know who you are?"

Morocco? I'd heard of it in the legends of Al-Andalus. What strange names they had! They were Arabian names, but it seemed that Agha and Kahyabak were military ranks.

"Of course I know who I am. I am Al-Baz Al-

Monqad, son of Al-Thib Al-Hakeem,[1] chieftain of the Sherokah clan."

"Is that one of the Andalucian clans?" he asked in a concerned and sympathetic tone that I could not understand.

I tensed up a bit when Hamzah returned with a worn-out piece of leather to show to Antarah, who examined it with clear interest. I knew exactly what was drawn on that leather; it was the map of Yaqteenya.

"What is this map? Where is Yaqteenya?" I feared that in my recklessness on this expedition, I would destroy Yaqteenya, and lead our enemy to it, instead of saving it from itself and the strife that was tearing it apart. I knew this could happen, but it was a risk that I had to face. The Moors left me no choice. I had to put an end to this strife. I had to find the evidence to prove or negate the Moors' claims before the civil war in Yaqteenya wiped out everyone and everything.

"I will not give you any information that will reveal my country," I said, as I turned my back to Agha Antarah, and sat down on the floor.

"Then you will stay here until we have the answers we are looking for. Hamzah, carry these boxes to my chambers so that I can carefully examine them," Antarah said. Then I heard movement near the wall where my ship's wreckage was. I thought

---

[1] Al-Thib Al-Hakeem—Translation: Wise Wolf.

soldiers were carrying the boxes to his room. This was very strange. How did I hear the call to prayer from the outside? This must have been an elaborate scheme to fool me. I must stay alert. No one must know how to reach Yaqteenya. The Moors were right. If they knew about us, they would send their troops to finish what they had started in Al-Andalus two hundred and ninety years ago. I had to escape this place and destroy everything that might reveal Yaqteenya's location, but how? I examined the cell door. The latch was held in place by a rusty iron lock. I could easily break it if I poured acid on it. I carried a full assortment of chemicals in my luggage. I looked over the wreckage piled in the court in front of me. The lighting was flickering and dim. I had to concentrate to make out the wreckage from that distance. I crossed my legs and placed my hands on my knees as I closed my eyes. I took a deep breath as I began to meditate as my master, Saqr Al-Akaber[1], taught me: "Baz, if you ever need to find something, you must first link your soul to Allah, knower of the unseen. To do so, you must clear your mind from anything but your love of Allah and your hope for his blessings, then praise him and seek his forgiveness, and when you feel the cleansing of your soul and the strength of your connection to him, recite his verses: (يَٰبُنَىَّ إِنَّهَآ إِن تَكُ مِثْقَالَ حَبَّةٍ مِّنْ خَرْدَلٍ فَتَكُن فِى صَخْرَةٍ أَوْ فِى ٱلسَّمَٰوَٰتِ أَوْ فِى ٱلْأَرْضِ يَأْتِ بِهَا

---

[1] Saqr Al-Akaber—Translation: Falcon of the Elites.

19

[1](ٱللَّهَ إِنَّ ٱللَّهَ لَطِيفٌ خَبِيرٌ) *O my son!, "If there be but the weight of a mustard-seed and it were hidden in a rock, or anywhere in the heavens or on earth, Allah will bring it forth, for Allah understands the finest mysteries, and is well acquainted with them.* Keep repeating it until you see your need through the eye of your mind in a way that you have never seen it before. At that moment, open your eyes and gaze upon your surroundings and you shall see what would lead you to it." I kept repeating what I recalled of praise to Allah. I do not know how much time had passed while I was in that state, but after a while, I felt my environment fading away, and I felt as if my soul had left my body, as I no longer felt either it or my senses. I started to remember my bag, which was filled with solutions and materials. It was an old leather bag, a gift from my grandfather when I got my first Ijazah[2] in chemistry. He told me it was his first chemical bag when he was a boy. My grandfather's name, Al-Akrab Al-Haleem[3] was written on its side in his handwriting, and its edges were worn. I would carry it from a thick, green rope. I opened the bag and saw its bottled contents. I moved in closer, as a fly hovering over the bottles. Everything seemed so gigantic. I could clearly see the markings that the glass maker made on bottles. I never noticed

---

[1] Surat Luqman, verse 16.

[2] Ijazah is a certification process similar to apprenticeship.

[3] Al-Akrab Al-Haleem—Translation: The patient scorpion.

before how accurate those markings were, or how proud he was at mastering his trade. This was what I wanted, to see it in a way that I had never seen it before. I needed to open my eyes. Nothing had changed. The court was still in the same dim flickering firelight. I looked over the wreckage and boxes again, and my gaze fell upon a thick green rope that seemed to be glowing from within the boxes. It was my bag, but how could I get it. I needed to make one of the guards bring it to me. I stood up and started moaning as I banged on the cell's bars. My knees weakened as I tried holding onto the bars to keep myself standing. I eventually fell to the ground while still banging on the bars, but my banging suddenly became weaker. I saw a guard's feet in front of my face on the other side of the bars.

"What is wrong with you?" he asked, clearly irritated with me.

"I am terminally ill, and I need my medicine," I said.

"Why would we care? Do we look like a hospice to you?" the guard asked me.

"I just need my medicine from that bag with the green rope," I said, as I pointed with my shaky hand toward the bag.

The guard looked in the direction that I was pointing. He moved slowly toward the bag, picked it up, opened it, and looked through its contents. "Careful! Don't break the bottles," I said, quite fearful. If he broke one of the acid bottles, it would eat into his hand and the bag.

He returned to my cell with the bag in his hand. He wore a smirk that I knew all too well. He was not planning to give me anything from that bag. I was almost certain that he was going to drop my medicine bottle to the floor to shatter it. Good! I could make use of this soldier's wickedness. I reached for the water pitcher.

"Which of these bottles has your medicine?"

"It is a blue bottle, almost as big as an apricot."

The soldier pulled out the bottle and shook it, as his smirk widened. He asked, "Is this it?"

"Yes, yes! Please take care and don't drop it. It's glass and it's fragile," I replied.

He looked at me, tauntingly, as he opened his palm, allowing the bottle to fall from his hand and shatter on the stone floor. He laughed as it shattered. That was exactly what I was waiting for. His laughter would force him to take in deep breaths of the rising smoke, so I pushed the pitcher toward my face, forcing the water to fill my nostrils. I believed the soldier thought I was about to throw up, as his giggles grew louder, until it suddenly stopped. I was not sure whether it was because he had noticed the smoke rising from the shattered bottle or from its effects on him! I raised my head, as I held my breath. The soldier collapsed, causing my bag to fall from his hands, speeding toward the stone ground. I extended my arms through the bars to catch it before it crashed

22

to the floor. Thank God! I succeeded in catching it just before the last of its contents shattered on the floor. I pulled the bag into my cell and went through it until I found what I wanted. I pulled out the acid bottle and poured a few drops onto the lock. Then I waited until I could break the lock.

A shadow appeared in the court, along with footsteps, which got faster as they approached my cell. I hid the bag underneath the wooden bed. The guy reached my cell and bent down on his knees, as he angrily yelled, "What happened here!?"

"I have no idea, Sir. He just collapsed," I replied.

"Do I look like a fool? Step away from the door," he said, as he held the lock to put the key in. He then screamed in pain. The acid must have passed through the lock. I jumped up, held the soldier's head, and pulled it quickly toward the bars. He screamed in pain as he tried to pull away, but I again pulled his head toward the bars, striking him unconscious this time. I pulled his sword from its sheath and struck the lock several times before it broke. It seemed that the place had but a few scattered soldiers; otherwise, someone would have heard all of the noise and come to investigate.

I pushed the cell door open and hurried toward what remained of my ship's wreckage. I went through the boxes, looking for my books and weapons, but could only find a second chemical bag with most of its bottles shattered. I picked up what remained and put them in my bag. I scattered some of my powders over

23

the wreckage, causing it to burn up in an attempt to hide any evidence it might have on the location of Yaqteenya. I returned to my cell and took a few pieces of onion from the food plate, then sped out of the yard, looking for Antarah's quarters, so that I might reclaim some of my things.

I found a locked, heavy wooden door. I crashed into it while holding a second bottle of the sleeping potion that took out the first soldier. Antarah was standing behind a wooden desk that was worn out by time and sea moisture. He was about to pick up his sword off the wall facing him.

"Don't you dare step forward to hold that sword!" I yelled.

"And how will you stop me?" he asked.

"I do not want to hurt anyone. Just let me take my things and leave in peace, marid," I said.

"Marid! You truly are mad. Who are you? And how did you get out of your cell?"

"I told you, I am Al-Baz Al-Monqad, son of Al-Thib Al-Hakeem, chieftain of the Sherokah clan. I can tell you no more than that," I said.

Antarah snarled with anger and swiftly moved toward his sword, and the moment he held it, he pointed it toward me, as he said, "Now, slowly move in front of me, as I return you to your cell."

"I apologize in advance for your headache," I said. Then I threw the bottle underneath Antarah's feet, and held an onion to my nose. Thick smoke rose *from the shattered bottle. Antarah looked at the smoke with wonder, then looked at me in overwhelming anger. He barely took one step toward me before collapsing on the ground. I moved toward the boxes, which were scattered around the room. I found another bag with bottles filled with liquids and sands of different colors. I took most of them and stuffed them into my bag. Then I moved to the desk, took my tools, a couple of scrolls, and a book, and piled the rest of the things on the desk over by the boxes.*

I examined the boxes until I found one with a trace of a partial falcon symbol. I kicked its base to open up a compartment with a sword and dagger, along with their carrying belts.

I pulled both of them out of their sheaths to inspect their blades' orange, slightly-goldish color. This was, in fact, my sword that my father gave me the day I became a man. I put the first belt around my waste, and the other over my shoulder and around my chest. I returned the dagger to its sheath on my shoulder and my sword on my waste. I pulled out a bottle with a blue liquid and another with black sand. I threw the black sand over the boxes, looked at Antarah, and said, "I am sorry, but you left me no choice." I then threw the second bottle, and the liquid turned into fire the moment it touched the scattered black sand. The fire spread across the wreckage. I lifted Antarah and pulled him outside.

I exited the building while pulling Antarah, as smoke rose from the building. The moment I got outside, I heard drums echoing from every direction, and heard a woman's voice yelling, "Father! Father!"

I looked with terror at the girl standing only a couple of steps away from me. She was carrying a book with a thick, leather cover, damaged by sea water, while part of the book's title, written in gold, shone in the firelight. "The guide for do--- in echos and sh--- …" This was the book I was looking for. I had to have it. I was about to grab it from her, but an arrow struck in the ground between us, and I heard a voice calling from afar, "He is here in the yard!"

I stood to run like the wind and vanish in the darkness. I glanced behind me to find Hamzah feeling for Antarah's pulse and heard him ask the woman, "Are you ok?"

"Yyyyess. How is my father?" she answered.

"He seems to be unconscious."

"Thank God, but what happened? Who was that man?" she asked.

"We do not know. All he said was that he was from the Sherokah clan."

"Who are the Sherokah clan?!" she asked.

(2)
Strife

Yasser Bahjatt ياسر بهجت

Friday the second of Shawal 290 FG

I opened my weary eyes from the annoying
knocking on our house's door. I pulled the pillow over
my head in hopes of blocking that sound from
reaching my ears so that I could go back to sleep. The
knocking got harder, as I resisted in utter laziness, the
urge to get out of bed to check the door. I thought that
surely someone else would take care of the noise. The
minutes passed and the clearly-nervous knocking
persisted. I rubbed my eyes as I yawned with
irritation over the knocker who had forced me to leave
my bed, where I was hoping to spend an entire lazy
day after the full Eid[1] day we had the day before. I
put on some clothes and left my room, looking right
and left, wondering why no one else had opened the
door. I reached the door while the knocker was still
knocking frenetically. I opened the door to vex the
knocker, who turned out to be the Khalifa's son, Fida
Al-Deen, who was about to stumble, as his fist was
headed toward my face. I held him at arm's length in
a defensive move, as I asked, jokingly, "What is
wrong with you Fida? You have forgotten everything
our master had taught us about balance in dealing

---

[1] Eid is the title for the two Islamic holidays. Eid Al-Fitr is the first
day of non-fasting after Ramadan, and Eid Al-Adha is the first day
after the Haj (pilgrimage).

29

with surprises."

Fida looked at me as he gathered his breath. His face was clearly tense, as he asked me, "Why have you not answered my knocking? Have you not heard what is going on?!"

"What happened? Did the sun rise from the west?[1]" I asked, clearly disregarding him as I stretched out my arms.

"I have no time for your lumpishness. This is serious. Put on some nice clothes and follow me to the palace," he said, as he raised himself to ride his horse. "The rumors are confirmed. A group of those who deny the existence of the old world have come forward publically," and with that, he sped off in the direction of the palace.

I noticed that no one else was home. Where had they all gone this early in the morning?! I went out to the yard to check the clock. It was still very early for Friday prayers. I sluggishly moved toward the dining room in hopes of catching a piece of dough before the rest of my family wiped it all out. Strange! I did not smell anything. I went to the dining room. The fire was not lit. Where was my mother? This was not like her. Friday breakfast was one of our family's rituals that my mother would never miss!! Where was everyone?!

Given my father's position and stature as the

---

[1] In Islamic texts, the major sign of the end of times is the sun rising from the west.

chieftain of the Sherokah clan, I had never been interested in the matters of state and people. I left those complicated matters to my father and elder brother, as I spent my time learning the arts of fighting, horseback riding, and war from the best knights, fighters, warriors, and heads of the army. I knew that lately, my father and brother had been discussing the people's whispering about the debate of the truth regarding the old world and the Moors. I, however, always found excuses to withdraw from such dialogue, especially when it intensified and one of them tried to embarrass me by asking for my opinion about the outcomes and effects of such rumors.

What Fida had just said must have something to do with everyone disappearing from home. The Khalifa must have sent for my father and he must have taken my brother along, as usual, as he was preparing him to become the chieftain of our clan. For my mother to go with them to the palace, however, meant that it was serious, and that she had gone to be with the Khalifa's wives. My mother was not only the wife of one of Yaqteenya's clan chieftains, but she was also the Khalifa's cousin, and had a long and strong relationship with his wife since childhood. But why would Fida ask me to follow them to the palace? I had nothing to do with such topics, and he had never asked me to come to the palace for anything other than chatting and sparring. I went back to bed, totally ignoring Fida. I knew this would make him mad, but I was sure I could make it up to him after Friday prayers by letting him beat me in our next duel. Try as I might, though, I couldn't get back to sleep, as curiosity snuck into my head and filled it with questions bordering on a headache. I could not resist. I had to know. I jumped out of bed and put on my formal suit, my sword and dagger, and ran toward the palace. It was not very far and the protocols to enter a horse into the palace stables were irritating and boring, but I am in a hurry.

When I reached the palace, Friday prayers were still hours away, but the palace's mosque was filled, and a lot of worshipers were still arriving at this early hour and sitting in the open areas around it. I sped up my steps, as I made my way through the crowds until I reached the palace gate, where one of the guards stopped me.

"Sorry, Baz. Entry into the palace is restricted today," he said.

"I am here by the personal invitation of Fida," I replied.

"I apologize, but my orders were clear and straight from the Khalifa. I am not to allow anyone in unless I am so informed by someone from the palace, and Fida has not told me to allow you in."

I disappeared back into the crowd. Everything that was going on fueled my curiosity. I had to get to the bay that overlooked the palace. A water path led into the palace walls. I did not think the guards would be watching it, for no one was crazy enough to *dive into the bay in that cold winter. I moved slowly so as to not alert any of the guards as I stepped into the bay. I then forced myself to dive in, even though I had the strongest urge to run away from the almost-freezing water. After swimming underwater for a minute or so, I came out in one of the palace's crypts that I know by heart. I came out of the crypt and hurried to the Khalifa's court. I arrived to the governing council that was filled with clan chieftains and a group of ministers, along with army commanders and police men. In the center was the Khalifa Al-Wadda, son of Sirat Al-Haq Al-Moori.[1] I was dripping wet and the steps of my two water-filled shoos echoed in the hall. Everyone stopped talking, as all eyes turned toward me. Fida's jaw dropped, so as to gaze at me in disbelief, while my father threw me a fiery look that only meant one thing: "I will kill you when we get home." I stopped moving, as I smiled stupidly and motioned to the Khalifa to continue speaking.*

As he looked to my father, the Khalifa said, "As I was saying before your son, Baz, interrupted us, the response to what the mobs did yesterday must be firm and swift."

"To respond to these crowds with force and soldiers will only add more smoke to this fire. These crowds were not moving with mere violence and destruction. They were driven by the complaint that

---

[1] Al-Wadda, son of Sirat Al-Haq Al- Moori—Translation: The Moorish who lights his surroundings, Son of the path of truth.

33

our Khalifa is based upon fraud," replied my father, as he stared at me, intensely angry, showing me how displeased he was that I showed up, at that time, in that shape.

"And what do you propose? Should we allow them to continue this chaos so that the commoners would think that the Khalifa does not have the means to stop the aggressors or punish the corrupt?"

"That was never what I advocated for, but punishment must be delivered to anyone who has done harm. At the same time, however, this problem must be dealt with and trust must be restored amongst the people. You must speak to them and remind them of the grace God has shown them since the day the Moors showed up."

Al-Muthana, the army's general, interrupted and said, "Speeches, dialogue, remind, and convince. Why show weakness? We have the power to deal with such people and make an example of them for all eternity. Where is your loyalty to the Khalifa, or is your loyalty to your kin, who are trying to destabilize his rule?"

The Khalifa slammed his fist on the table they had all gathered around, and said, furious, "Enough! There you are, Muthana, fueling the problem from within my court! How dare you question the loyalty of our wise man or any of my subjects in my presence or even in my absence? Sherokah's wise man is right in his advice and fears. I must speak to my subjects *and remind them of the blessings of safety and security that God has bestowed upon us all."*

I had no idea what had gotten into me. I was smarter than to speak in the Khalifa's court in the presence of my father without first being spoken to or asked, but for reasons known only to God Himself, I spoke. "But why does the Khalifa not send someone to cross the Okeanós and return with the decisive evidence to quell all of the skeptics' doubts?!"

Silence engulfed the room, as everyone stared at me in astonishment, as my father's face went red and my brother lowered his head, and Fida put his hands on top of his head, as he was shocked in disbelief at what I had just done. I think, at that moment, he regretted asking me to come. No one dared utter a word. Time stopped, or very nearly so. It felt like a lifetime passed in that deafening silence, and then, suddenly, the Khalifa giggled out loud.

"And the eagle strikes again!"

He looked at my father, as he continued. "I admire your son's courage and candor. I am sure that many of those present today are asking themselves the same question, although they already know the answer, especially those of your kin."

My father looked at me with obvious disappointment, as he replied, "Oh, Khalifa, of the believers, he is but a young, reckless boy, who has not yet learned the art of holding one's tongue and weighing one's words. I assure you that I shall punish him myself, and severely so. Come, Baz. Apologize to the Khalifa for your impudence."

The Khalifa replied, while still smiling, "Do not concern yourself, oh wise man. His question was the same question as that of the rest of my subjects, and it deserves an answer, but he must wait to hear it, along with the rest of his brothers. I will speak to my subjects today, in accordance with your advice, oh wise man. Now, all of you leave me, save for our wise man and writer, so I can prepare my speech."

"Nice job, Baz. You have embarrassed our father once again," said my older brother, Al-Asad Al-Saboor,[1] as he made his way out of the palace.

"I know it is tradition to bathe before Friday prayer, but to bathe while in one's full formal outfit is something I know of no reference to."

I turned to find Fida trying hard to hold in his laughter. "Very funny! I hold you fully responsible for this. You forgot to tell the guards to let me into the palace!"

Fida's laughter stopped, as his face changed color. "I apologize for that. I was in a hurry," Fida said.

"And the result was that I embarrassed my father and made him the joke of the counsel. My father will never forgive me for this. You owe me."

"Again, I apologize. I confess this was my doing. I do owe you. Ask for anything you want. Come to my room and dry yourself off before prayer."

"I accept your apology, and I will hold onto that

---

[1] Al-Asad Al-Saboor—Translation: The Patient Lion.

favor. This is the opportunity of a lifetime, to hold the Khalifa's son in my debt." Then I said, in a hurry, "Let us see who makes it to your room first," as I ran like the wind. Fida's room was on the other side of the palace, three stories up. This had been our habit since we were kids. This race of ours was a catastrophe with which the palace workers were all too familiar, as we jumped from floor to floor and fell over one of them, or slid on the smooth marble floor under their arms, as they carried trays of food and drinks. Fida won this time, but that is all right, as I am still in the lead.

❖⟡⟡⟡⟡⟡⟡⟡⟡❖

Fida and I entered the Mosque from the front entrance, near the mihrab, where the Imam usually enters. All eyes were raised toward us in anticipation, then went back to reading the Quran when they did not find the Khalifa amongst us. We sat in the front row, along with a group of chieftains, although I had seen the crowds outside the mosque. I did not expect all of the worshipers inside, as the mosque was over-crowded. You could barely find a place to stand. The location we sat in was surrounded by guards, who denied worshipers access to that area, to make room for the Khalifa's guests. If it weren't for those guards, we would have had to pray in the far edges of the Mosque's outer yards. We each picked up a copy of the holy Quran as we sat down and read. I finished

Surat Al-Kahf[1] and followed it with two full sections. Noon time was almost over and the Khalifa had yet to show up.

I felt the worshipers fidget from waiting, then the front door was opened and all eyes went up again. I saw my father enter, followed by the Khalifa. My father moved in to sit amongst the other chieftains, while the Khalifa stepped up to the platform and spoke. "Alsalamu alikum wa rahmatu allahi wa barakatuh,"[2] then he sat down.

The muezzin[3] called for the prayer. The moments of his call passed heavy on everyone, as they waited for the Khalifa's speech with drained patience. Even the muezzin's call was different that day than at any other time. He did not stretch out his call, as usual. His performance was clearly rushed, and when he was done, silence engulfed the mosque. Everyone was anticipating the Khalifa's speech, everyone, that is, other that the Khalifa himself. The Khalifa was mumbling to himself. I have no idea whether he was praising Allah or reviewing what he was about to say, but time was passing and the Khalifa was still sitting.

And then, finally, the Khalifa stood and said, "Praise be to Allah, whose praise completes our

---

[1] Surat Al-Kahf is the 18th chapter of the holy Quran. Loosely translated, "The Chapter of the cave," it is customary to read it every Friday.

[2] Loosely translated to, "May God's peace, mercy, and blessings fall upon you."

[3] Muezzin is the one who calls for the prayers.

blessings. Prayers and blessings go out to his most noble creation, Mohammad, son of Abdullah, his final prophet and messenger. I seek refuge in Allah from the evils of ourselves and our bad deeds. He who is guided by Allah is on the true path, and he who Allah misleads shall not find a savior guide, almightily said in his holy book: (وَٱعْتَصِمُواْ بِحَبْلِ ٱللَّهِ جَمِيعًا

وَلَا تَفَرَّقُواْ وَٱذْكُرُواْ نِعْمَتَ ٱللَّهِ عَلَيْكُمْ إِذْ كُنتُمْ أَعْدَآءً فَأَلَّفَ بَيْنَ قُلُوبِكُمْ فَأَصْبَحْتُم بِنِعْمَتِهِۦٓ إِخْوَٰنًا وَكُنتُمْ عَلَىٰ شَفَا حُفْرَةٍ مِّنَ ٱلنَّارِ فَأَنقَذَكُم مِّنْهَاۗ كَذَٰلِكَ يُبَيِّنُ ٱللَّهُ لَكُمْ ءَايَٰتِهِۦ لَعَلَّكُمْ تَهْتَدُونَ)[1]

And hold fast, all together, by the Allah's rope, and be not divided among yourselves; and remember with gratitude Allah's favor on you; for ye were enemies and He joined your hearts in love, so that by His Grace, ye became brethren; and ye were on the brink of the pit of Fire, and He saved you from it. Thus doth Allah make His Signs clear to you That ye may be guided. Brethren of faith, let each one of us look upon his right and his left, in front of him and behind him. Allah has bestowed this favor on us today. He has gathered us on this virtuous day in his obedience. He has gathered us as brothers in love and support to worship him and pray to him. These great masses that have gathered here today are evidence of our love of and for one another, and our fear of a strife that separates us from our Muslim brethren. Today, my brethren believers, I shall remind you of

---

[1] Surat Al Imran verse 103.

Allah's blessings on us all. I owe you no favors, nor do you owe me any. Allah alone is the one who has bestowed favors upon all of us with this, Brethren. We all share love and intimacy. My grandfather, Ali, son of Saad, came to you as an immigrant, fleeing, with his faith, from Al-Andalus. He and those with him came to this land of yours hungry after they had been lost at sea for months, and all the food they had was gone. They came to your land, and the first thing they found was the Yaqreen[1] plant, upon which they fed. It saved them, as it did the prophet Jonah—peace be upon him—before. So they took it as a sign of rejoicing, in anticipation of this good land. Yes, Allah had blessed them, and you, that they had landed on this blessed land, to build this very mosque, almost three centuries ago. They came to you and found your warring tribes, and when your ancestors knew of their arrival, they fell upon them from every direction. Thirty years besieged within the walls of this city that my ancestors had built, thirty years of continuous war, as the Moorish knights defended what remained of the league of Islam. They were much more advanced in war techniques and weaponry than the people of these blessed lands then. They could have killed an extraordinary number of them with the excuse of defending themselves, their families, and their religion, but they did not step a single foot outside these city walls. Instead, they sent

---

[1] Yaqteen is the Arabic name for pumpkin.

40

messengers to the chieftains of your clans, despite their struggles while under siege. They were afraid and homesick, yet they did not forget their higher calling in this life, so they spread Allah's religion and invited them to Islam. Some believed and others did not, and with time, the clans joined Islam en mass. Pacts and treaties were established, and you became brothers by the blessing of Allah. The Moors did not seek to rule the clans, but treated them with kindness. This, as well as the justice and brotherhood they had setup between the clans, made them pledge their allegiance to my grandfather, Mohammad the twelfth, as a Khalifa amongst all of them. Gathering all the tribal flags under one unifying flag of Islam, one of the most important conditions of that pledge was that no one should ever go back to the old world, so that the enemies of Allah's religion would not know of us. In return, the Moors had spread science and religion to all corners of Yaqteenya, to build together a civilization greater than that of old Andalus."

The Khalifa sat down to catch his breath between the two speeches. Then he began again. "My brethren in Allah, some corrupters are trying to demolish what our grandparents built throughout the last three centuries. They want to start a conflict that would break the bonds of brotherhood and love not only between the Moors and Yaqteenyans, but also between all brethren. Do not fall for such tactics, and hold on to Allah's rope. Those behind this strategy claim that we, the Moors, have lied to you about Allah's religion,

41

that we have only used it to rule over you, and that the law of isolating the old world was fraudulently set up by us to deceive you and hide the truth."

He then looked toward my father before continuing. "From this platform, I testify to you and to Allah, that I and any of those with me, carry only love, loyalty, and brotherhood for all of you, and that we only want what is good for you. Allah has blessed us all with more than two centuries of peace, away from the strife of war, and what I fear the most is that this strife ignites the fires of war again, or that the breaking of the law of isolating the old world would bring its fires from there. For this reason, after much discussion with our wise men, the chieftains of the clans, I have decided to maintain the bonds of brotherhood that have grown between us all and relieve the people of Yaqteenya from a pledge that had passed almost two and a half centuries ago. We are mere guests upon this land, and you have shown us great hospitality and generous accommodations. You may pledge your allegiance to whomever you want. Start the prayers."

With that, the Khalifa stepped down from the platform and the muezzin called for the start of prayer. The mosque was engulfed in a sad hue. Its echo could be heard in the crying voice of the muezzin.

The Khalifa stood to lead us in prayer. He read in the first set:

وَٱعْتَصِمُواْ بِحَبْلِ ٱللَّهِ جَمِيعًا وَلَا تَفَرَّقُواْ وَٱذْكُرُواْ نِعْمَتَ ٱللَّهِ)

42

عَلَيْكُمْ إِذْ كُنتُمْ أَعْدَآءً فَأَلَّفَ بَيْنَ قُلُوبِكُمْ فَأَصْبَحْتُم بِنِعْمَتِهِۦٓ إِخْوَٰنًا

وَكُنتُمْ عَلَىٰ شَفَا حُفْرَةٍ مِّنَ ٱلنَّارِ فَأَنقَذَكُم مِّنْهَا ۗ كَذَٰلِكَ يُبَيِّنُ ٱللَّهُ لَكُمْ

ءَايَـٰتِهِۦ لَعَلَّكُمْ تَهْتَدُونَ) [1] *And hold fast, all together, by*
the Allah's rope, and be not divided among
yourselves; and remember with gratitude Allah's favor
on you; for ye were enemies and He joined your
hearts in love, so that by His Grace, ye became
brethren; and ye were on the brink of the pit of Fire,
and He saved you from it. Thus doth Allah make His
Signs clear to you that ye may be guided.

Then in the second set, he read:

(وَإِن طَآئِفَتَانِ مِنَ ٱلْمُؤْمِنِينَ ٱقْتَتَلُوا۟ فَأَصْلِحُوا۟ بَيْنَهُمَا ۖ فَإِنۢ بَغَتْ

إِحْدَىٰهُمَا عَلَى ٱلْأُخْرَىٰ فَقَٰتِلُوا۟ ٱلَّتِى تَبْغِى حَتَّىٰ تَفِىٓءَ إِلَىٰٓ أَمْرِ ٱللَّهِ ۚ فَإِن

فَآءَتْ فَأَصْلِحُوا۟ بَيْنَهُمَا بِٱلْعَدْلِ وَأَقْسِطُوٓا۟ ۖ إِنَّ ٱللَّهَ يُحِبُّ ٱلْمُقْسِطِينَ ۞

إِنَّمَا ٱلْمُؤْمِنُونَ إِخْوَةٌ فَأَصْلِحُوا۟ بَيْنَ أَخَوَيْكُمْ ۚ وَٱتَّقُوا۟ ٱللَّهَ لَعَلَّكُمْ

تُرْحَمُونَ ۞ يَـٰٓأَيُّهَا ٱلَّذِينَ ءَامَنُوا۟ لَا يَسْخَرْ قَوْمٌ مِّن قَوْمٍ عَسَىٰٓ أَن يَكُونُوا۟

خَيْرًا مِّنْهُمْ وَلَا نِسَآءٌ مِّن نِّسَآءٍ عَسَىٰٓ أَن يَكُنَّ خَيْرًا مِّنْهُنَّ ۖ وَلَا تَلْمِزُوٓا۟

أَنفُسَكُمْ وَلَا تَنَابَزُوا۟ بِٱلْأَلْقَٰبِ ۖ بِئْسَ ٱلِٱسْمُ ٱلْفُسُوقُ بَعْدَ ٱلْإِيمَٰنِ ۚ وَمَن

لَّمْ يَتُبْ فَأُو۟لَـٰٓئِكَ هُمُ ٱلظَّٰلِمُونَ ۞ يَـٰٓأَيُّهَا ٱلَّذِينَ ءَامَنُوا۟ ٱجْتَنِبُوا۟ كَثِيرًا

مِّنَ ٱلظَّنِّ إِنَّ بَعْضَ ٱلظَّنِّ إِثْمٌ ۖ وَلَا تَجَسَّسُوا۟ وَلَا يَغْتَب بَّعْضُكُم بَعْضًا ۚ

أَيُحِبُّ أَحَدُكُمْ أَن يَأْكُلَ لَحْمَ أَخِيهِ مَيْتًا فَكَرِهْتُمُوهُ ۚ وَٱتَّقُوا۟ ٱللَّهَ ۚ إِنَّ

ٱللَّهَ تَوَّابٌ رَّحِيمٌ ۞ يَـٰٓأَيُّهَا ٱلنَّاسُ إِنَّا خَلَقْنَٰكُم مِّن ذَكَرٍ وَأُنثَىٰ

وَجَعَلْنَٰكُمْ شُعُوبًا وَقَبَآئِلَ لِتَعَارَفُوٓا۟ ۚ إِنَّ أَكْرَمَكُمْ عِندَ ٱللَّهِ أَتْقَىٰكُمْ

---

[1] Surat Aal Imran verse 103.

43

إِنَّ ٱللَّهَعَلِيمٌ خَبِيرٌ ۞ قَالَتِ ٱلْأَعْرَابُ ءَامَنَّا قُل لَّمْ تُؤْمِنُوا۟ وَلَـٰكِن قُولُوٓا۟ أَسْلَمْنَا وَلَمَّا يَدْخُلِ ٱلْإِيمَـٰنُ فِى قُلُوبِكُمْ وَإِن تُطِيعُوا۟ ٱللَّهَ وَرَسُولَهُۥ لَا يَلِتْكُم مِّنْ أَعْمَـٰلِكُمْ شَيْـًٔا إِنَّ ٱللَّهَ غَفُورٌ رَّحِيمٌ ۞ إِنَّمَا ٱلْمُؤْمِنُونَ ٱلَّذِينَ ءَامَنُوا۟ بِٱللَّهِ وَرَسُولِهِۦ ثُمَّ لَمْ يَرْتَابُوا۟ وَجَـٰهَدُوا۟ بِأَمْوَٰلِهِمْ وَأَنفُسِهِمْ فِى سَبِيلِ ٱللَّهِ أُو۟لَـٰٓئِكَ هُمُ ٱلصَّـٰدِقُونَ ۞ قُلْ أَتُعَلِّمُونَ ٱللَّهَ بِدِينِكُمْ وَٱللَّهُ يَعْلَمُ مَا فِى ٱلسَّمَـٰوَٰتِ وَمَا فِى ٱلْأَرْضِ وَٱللَّهُ بِكُلِّ شَىْءٍ عَلِيمٌ ۞ يَمُنُّونَ عَلَيْكَ أَنْ أَسْلَمُوا۟ قُل لَّا تَمُنُّوا۟ عَلَىَّ إِسْلَـٰمَكُم بَلِ ٱللَّهُ يَمُنُّ عَلَيْكُمْ أَنْ هَدَىٰكُمْ لِلْإِيمَـٰنِ إِن كُنتُمْ صَـٰدِقِينَ ۞ إِنَّ ٱللَّهَ يَعْلَمُ غَيْبَ ٱلسَّمَـٰوَٰتِ وَٱلْأَرْضِ وَٱللَّهُ بَصِيرٌۢ بِمَا تَعْمَلُونَ [1]*If two parties among the believers fall into a quarrel, make ye peace between them, but if one of them transgresses beyond bounds against the other, then fight ye (all) against the one that transgresses until it complies with the command of Allah; but if it complies, then make peace between them with justice, and be fair ● The believers are but a single brotherhood, so make peace and reconciliation between your two (contending) brothers; and fear Allah, that ye may receive Mercy. ● O ye who believe! let not a group (of men) scoff at another group, it may well be that the latter (at whom they scoff) are better than they; nor let a group of women scoff at another group, it may well be that the latter are better than they. And do not taunt one another, nor revile one another by nicknames. It is an evil*

---

[1] Surat Alhujurat verses 9-18

thing to gain notoriety for ungodliness after belief.
Those who do not repent are indeed the wrong-doers
● O ye who believe! Avoid suspicion as much (as
possible) for suspicion in some cases is a sin. Do not
spy, nor backbite one another. Would any of you like
to eat the flesh of his dead brother? You would surely
detest it. Have fear of Allah. Surely Allah is much
prone to accept repentance, is Most Compassionate ●
O mankind! We created you from a single (pair) of a
male and a female, and made you into nations and
tribes, that ye may know each other. Verily, the most
honored of you in the sight of Allah is (he who is) the
most righteous of you. And Allah has full knowledge
and is well acquainted (with all things). ● The desert
Arabs say, "We believe." Say, "Ye have no faith; but
ye (only) say, 'We have submitted our wills to Allah,'
For not yet has Faith entered your hearts. But if ye
obey Allah and His Messenger, He will not belittle
aught of your deeds for Allah is Oft-Forgiving, Most
Merciful." ● Only those are Believers who have
believed in Allah and His Messenger, and have never
since doubted, but have strived with their belongings
and their persons in the Cause of Allah. Such are the
sincere ones. ● Say "What! Will ye instruct Allah
about your religion? But Allah knows all that is in
the heavens and on earth ● They impress on thee as a
favor that they have embraced Islam. Say, "Count not
your Islam as a favor upon me. Nay, Allah has

conferred a favor upon you that He has guided you to the faith, if ye be true and sincere. ● Verily, Allah knows the secrets of the heavens and the earth: and Allah sees well all that ye do.

◦✧✧✧✧✧✧✧✧◦

The moment the Khalifa finished his prayer, voices rose with the name of the Khalifa. "We maintain our pledge, we pledge to Al-Wadda, we pledge to Al-Wadda.

And with the calls of the crowds, the chieftains of the tribes stood to pledge their allegiance to Al-Wadda as the Khalifa and renew the pact. When the chieftains were done and stood behind the Khalifa, everyone noticed that five chieftains were still standing where they were after prayer and had not pledged to the Khalifa. They were: Jabal, son of Siraa,[1] chieftain of the Nafojah clan; Al-Thawr Al-Samid, son of Al-Thalab Al-Hakeem,[2] chieftain of the Abatshah clan; Al-Aasid, son of Thiyab,[3] chieftain of the Comanish clan; Al-Hakam, son of Raad,[4] chieftain of the Aajeeb clan; and Haql, son of Sabr Al-Sama,[5] chieftain of the Shiyoon clan.

---

[1] Jabal, son of Siraa—Translation: Mountain son of Struggle.

[2] Al-Thawr Al-Samid, son of Al-Thalab Al-Hakeem—Translation: The staunch bull son of the wise fox.

[3] Al-Aasid, son of Thiyab—Translation: The Lioner son of Wolves.

[4] Al-Hakam, son of Raad—Translation: The Judge son of Thunder.

[5] Haql, son of Sabr Al-Sama—Translation: Field son of Sky's Patience.

Jabal stepped toward the Khalifa. Silence spread through the mosque, as everyone held their breath in anticipation of what would happen next. The Khalifa's soldiers were clearly tense, as their fists squeezed the hilts of their swords in anticipation. The Khalifa signaled them to be at ease. Jabal looked long into the eyes of the Khalifa, and then said, "As for me, I will not accept the rule of the Moors over us after this day.

"And who would rule Yaqteenya? You?" asked Bahr, son of Riyah,[1] chieftain of the Shawon clan.

Jabal ignored him, as he turned his back to the Khalifa, gazing upon the crowds. He spoke again. "Assembly of Yaqteenyans, I address you today on behalf of my tribe, Nafojah, and the tribes of Abatshah, Comanish, Aajeeb, and Shiyoon. We shall not pledge our allegiance to the Moors' Khalifa, nor shall we adhere to his commands after this day. Their control over us again from our land has lasted far too long, yet, out of respect for our ancestors, and the sacred[2] months, we shall allow the Moors, until Safar, to leave Yaqteenya. The age of superstition has ended, and we all know that there is not land across this Okeanós, save for the imagination of the Moors. Whoever among you would want to join us, we shall set camp west of the Abatshah Mountains until this

---

[1] Bahr, son of Riyah—Translation: Sea son of winds.

[2] The Muslims' sacred months are Thul Qidah, Thul Hijjah, Moharram, and Rajab. During these months, Muslims are not allowed to bear arms, except to defend themselves.

47

deadline. After that, we shall march onto new Qurtuba to wipe out every Moor in Yaqteenya, along with everyone who follows them or supports them or even believes in their religion."

Jabal moved swiftly and firmly out of the mosque, and behind him were the other four clan chieftains, followed by a substantial group of worshipers. With their exit, voices rose and intensified. Then words became a struggle that swept the entire mosque. The guards surrounded the Khalifa to protect him as they led him out of the mosque to his palace.

I stood in disbelief, as I watched my brethren fight each other as far as I could see. I could not believe that fighting would return to this land after more than two centuries, since the battle of New Qurtuba, which had reached all the way inside of this mosque. I must find a solution. This trouble must stop.

(3)

Akadeer

ياسر بهجت Yasser Bahjatt

The mid of Jumad the former 291 FG

Sixteen days have passed since I escaped my imprisonment. It was a full moon last night. I still cannot make out the days of the week. I've spent many days searching the coastline in hopes that I would find some of my things that the Okeanós' waves might have dragged as it had dragged me. That was no simple task, as the marid's scouts are still looking for me and I had to hide under the desert's sands more than once.

I found a few boxes of wreckage during the past few nights—some had supplies, a water goatskin, as well as my cape that had been gifted to me by my master, Saqr Al-Akaber, but it was somewhat torn and needs repair before it could return to its usual performance. I also found a few of my weapons that I will surely need in this mission, as well as a substantial amount of dinars[1] and dirhams[2].

I found a very small cave on the cliff of a mountain overlooking the Okeanós. It barely had enough room for me to lay down. It was hidden by a few boulders. It also had a slight breeze, making it a perfect place to shelter myself from the sun and scouts' eyes during the day. I could also watch the Okeanós

---

[1] A Dinar is a gold coin.
[2] A Dirham is a silver coin.

from here, hoping that I would see wreckage from my
ship. I shall wait here until tonight, and then I will
slip through the night's darkness and use the moon's
light to guide me in my journey.

The sun started to set. I carried my large bundle
filled with stuff I had collected in the last few days. I
was about to leave the cave, and before I came out
from behind the boulders, a black horse, as black as
the night, came running in the horizon on the line
separating the Okeanós from the land. Riding it was
a knight who was as black as the horse. A black cape
waved behind him. He must have been a second
marid, looking for me. I hid behind the boulder to
watch the marid. He was combing the Okeanós with
his eyes, as if searching for something. If he was not
searching for me, then what was he looking for?! The
horse suddenly stopped, and the knight put his hand
above his eyes, inspecting the horizon. I raised my
eyes to where he was looking. There was a mass of
logs and a human body was hanging onto it. This
person must be one of the passengers on my ship. The
horse moved into the Okeanós, toward the survivor,
while its knight urged it to hurry. For a brief
moment, I contemplated following him to help that
Yaqteenyan before he fell into captivity, but I
stopped, as this seemed most suspicious. How did this
marid know where to find this survivor? And why
was he not accompanied by many guards like
Antarah did when he found me? I moved closer, while

staying out of sight from the knight. I would be close enough to try and understand what was going on, and to help the Yaqteenyan, if I needed to. The knight arrived at the logs, tied them with a rope, and returned to the beach with them in tow. He jumped off his horse, stepped into the water to carry the survivor on his shoulder, and then easily threw him onto the beach. He went down on his knees, placed his ear on the man's chest to listen for a heartbeat, watched to see if the man's chest moved up and down, and placed his hand in front of the man's mouth to feel for air coming from the man, which would indicate that he was breathing. Then the man coughed. The marid jumped at the surprise. Then he giggled with a voice that echoed throughout the mountains, slapped the survivor's shoulder with his palm, and said, "You truly are stubborn, having survived the efforts of the angel of death, Himr."[1]

With that, I thought I saw the man raise his head and mumble something to the marid. I did not hear what he said, but it made the marid giggle again. The marid then carried the man whom he called Himr and placed him on the horse's back. He took hold of the horse's rein and led him south, back the way they came. I tried to move closer without the marid noticing me, to try to distinguish the survivor's features. He had long white hair. I could not make out his face from that distance, but he surely was not

---

[1] Himr—Translation: Comes from the word Ahmar, meaning red, loosely translated to reddish.

one of the ship's crew. Who was he, I wondered? How does this marid know him? I must follow them to figure out this relationship. I must maintain Yaqteenya's secret.

◦❖❖❖❖❖❖❖◦

We arrived at a great city at the end of the mountain range adjacent to the Okeanós. Its stone walls were at least a hundred arms tall, and in some places close to the mountain, it was more like two hundred arms. The sun was coming up from behind the city. The marid moved toward the mountain, followed by his horse. Even though the mountain terrain was very rough, the horse moved with ease and flexibility. It was as if they were walking over a previously-paved path that was almost invisible to those who did not know of its existence. The marid stopped in front of a huge rock at the point where the city walls met the mountain. There was no more room to move forward. He started to inspect the location, ensuring no one was watching him, so I hid behind the mountain's edge. I listened carefully, trying to figure out what he was doing there, as well as ensure he did not see me and was not moving toward me. I heard the sound of moving and falling rocks where the marid was standing. He must have been trying to climb the walls, but why? And what would he do with his horse and its rider? I waited for a few seconds, then the sounds completely stopped. I poked

my head out of my hiding place to see what was
going on, but I could not see any trace of the marid or
his horse, and the giant rock was hanging a few arms
above ground and moving slowly to hide a narrow
path. I moved quickly to enter the path before the
rock hid it again. I squeezed myself through the
remaining tight space, entering the tunnel right
before the rock closed up behind me and darkness
shaded the place, save for a small light at the end. I
followed the path to the end, only to find myself in
one of the city's noisy alleys. I looked left and right to
glimpse the marid's horse at the end of the alley. I
made my way through traffic, following the horse
from one alley to another, until we arrived at an old
house. He opened the stable gates and led the horse
inside. He then looked down both sides of the alley
before shutting the gate behind him.

◆✦✦✦✦✦✦✦✦◆

I had to stay and keep an eye on this house to
find a way to save the Yaqteenyan from the marid,
but first I had to get to know my surroundings, to
know its ins and outs by heart. I wandered the alleys
until I arrived at a spacious court that seemed to be
one of the city's markets. It was a good place to find a
leather merchant to fix my cape. I roamed the market
listening to people's chatter. The city's name was
Akadeer. It was primarily a military city, as the
navy filled its harbor with thousands of soldiers and

sailors. I was amazed that the majority there spoke
Arabic, but their accents were different from what I
was used to in Yaqteenya. Even stranger was that
they also used dinars and dirhams in their dealings. I
found a leather merchant and browsed through his
products until I found what I was looking for.

"How much is this piece?"

"Eleven dirhams."

I took out the dirhams and handed them to the
merchant, and was about to move away with the
piece in hand, but the merchant put his hand on top
of it and stopped me. "Wait, I have never seen the
likes of these dirhams before. Where are you from?
Your tongue is strange to me."

"I am a passerby, and those are the only dirhams
I have. Take them, if you wish, or return them to me
and I will find someone else who will accept them," I
said.

The merchant gazed long and hard into my eyes,
then inspected the dirhams once more, then signaled
me to leave. I picked up the leather piece and moved
on to inspect the rest of the market. I noticed the
merchant watching me, and when he thought I no
longer noticed him, he closed his shop in a hurry, and
moved toward a group of soldiers who were roaming
the market. He spoke to them as he occasionally gave
me looks of suspicion. Then he pulled a shiny object
out of his pocket (I think it was one of the dirhams I
gave him) and pointed toward me. The soldiers

fidgeted nervously and then they started moving in my direction. They pushed people out of their way, and I slowly moved away from them, toward one of the alleys, acting as if I had not noticed them heading in my direction. I heard their voices, as they quarreled with the shoppers they had pushed after I disappeared in the alley, and when they arrived to its entrance, there was no trace of me. Their captain yelled in anger, "Where did he go?!"

The soldiers looked around in search of any clue, and then their captain commanded them to search for me. I was watching them from the roof of one of the buildings, where I had climbed and hid just before they got there. I stayed put for some time to make sure they were not around. I had to return to where that marid had taken the Yaqteenyan old man. I had to help him.

ياسر بهجت Yasser Bahjatt

(4)

My Totem

Yasser Bahjatt ياسر بهجت

يقطينيا Yaqteenya

Sunday the twenty-ninth of Thul Hijjah 290 FG

I prayed Fajur[1] in New Qurtuba's mosque, along
with my father and older brother. The Khalifa's
messenger went to my father yesterday after Isha
prayer, and informed him that the Khalifa wanted to
meet us after Fajur prayer immediately. The Khalifa
led the prayer, as he usually did. There has not been a
day where he did not lead the prayers in Qurtuba's
mosque, except on the occasions when he visits one of
the far regions or if he was sick, although the head of
his guards insisted that he should stay in his palace in
fear that someone might try to assassinate him, and
the Khalifa's response was always, "I do not know
Jabal to be one who betrays a pact." After prayer, the
Khalifa signaled to my father for us to follow him to
the palace. Fida was in his company. When we
arrived to the Khalifa's court, Fida stopped us and
signaled the guards to close the doors behind my
father. Then we waited outside the court. As time
passed, the chieftains of the other clans loyal to the
Khalifa began arriving, along with their advisors, but
Fida insisted that they should also wait until the
Khalifa asked for them. After a long while, the court's

---

[1] Muslims pray five times a day: Fajur, just before dawn; Thuhur, at
noon; Asor, in the afternoon when the sun is midway in its descent;
Maghrib, when the sun sets; and Isha, at night.

61

door was opened and my father appeared. He signaled to the clan chieftains and their advisors to enter, followed by my brother, but my father stopped me and Fida, and said, "Not yet," and closed the door behind him.

Worry crept into Fida's eyes, and he began pacing back and forth in front of the court's door. As for me, I just sat on one of the sofas scattered in front of the court, and leaned my head backward. I had barely dozed off when Fida shoved me and asked, "How can you sleep at a time like this?"

"A time like what, exactly?" I asked.

"Do you not know that the deadline given to us by Jabal is but a few days away, and then the first war between the tribes of Yaqteenya in two and a half centuries will start? Are you not even the least bit concerned?"

"Why should I be concerned when I can do nothing about it? And where is your trust in your father's leadership abilities? Where is your trust in my father's wisdom? Trust me, there is nothing to worry about or to be concerned over. They are gathered in there now with the clans' chieftains and will emerge any moment with a brilliant strategic plan to end this conflict."

"A brilliant strategic plan to end this conflict?! It's that simple to you? Oh, what a dreamer you are, Baz."

I shook my head and rolled my eyes, in mockery,

and returned to my nap. But, my miserable luck would not allow me such luxury, as the moment I dozed off again, the sound of the opening court door echoed. Fida kicked my foot to make me stand. Bahr, son of Riyah, chieftain of the Shawon clan, was standing in the door looking at us. Fida was practically frozen right where he stood, while I sat up on the sofa. Bahr did not seem pleased, as he shifted his gaze between me and Fida, until he said, "The Khalifa wants to talk to both of you."

I followed Fida in and heard the door shut behind me. I was baffled by the Khalifa's request to speak to me. I do not recall the Khalifa ever requesting my presence or even talking to me, aside from the passing greeting when he happened to meet me while I was in the company of Fida or my father. But to address me willingly, this would definitely be a first. I wondered what the Khalifa wanted from me. Was he still upset over my entrance to his court dripping with water? And why today, after all of this time? My eyes swept the audiences' faces in worry; bafflement covered my face, as I tried to read my father's expressions in hopes of understanding what was going on, but I couldn't get anything. I almost slammed into Fida as he stopped in the center of the court, and I noticed that the Khalifa had focused his sight on us.

"Baz, from what I recall, raptors were your totem, and your master is Saqr Al-Akaber. Is that correct?" the Khalifa asked me.

My astonishment increased as I answered, "Yes,

Sir, that is correct."

"And what is your master's assessment of your totem mastery?" asked the Khalifa.

"He says that my mastery is beyond three black feathers, and that I am about to add a white feather to it. Also that my communication ability with them is beyond what most thought possible." I could not control my confusion any more. "I'm sorry, Sir, but I do not recall you ever showing an interest in my abilities or teachings before now. If I may be so bold, why the sudden interest?"

The Khalifa laughed out loud and replied, "I am interested in all of my subjects, but I am particularly interested in my son's friends." The Khalifa then looked at my father and said, "I know you still have reservations regarding what I need your son to do, but, as you know, I am not only risking your son, but I need to send my own son, as well, and this is why I prefer your son over all other raptors." He looked back at me, only to see confusion on my face, and then he continued. "Baz, as you know, masses have gathered at the Abatshah mountains, and I am afraid that we will have to face our brothers in a few days. I do not want to face them without knowing their numbers and armament, so I need someone to scout the gathering and return that information to our army as quickly as possible. As you know, the best scouts are the raptor and deer totems, and since Fida's totem is deer, I insisted that he be one of the scouts. I need a *raptor to join him, which is where you come in. I also need to show everyone that Moors and Yaqteenyans are working together, and that their leaders are on the front lines."*

The Khalifa stopped talking and signaled to Al-Muthana, the Army General, who led us to a table on one side of the court. Yaqteenya's map was spread out on top of it. He pointed to the Abatshah Mountain and said, *"Abatshah Mountain is a twenty-day walk from here. We shall set camp at Al-Oyoon Al-Hamia,[1] near the Oshata forests here, almost mid-way. I cannot stress enough the importance of the information you will gather. If you are as good as I believe you are, then you are our best shot to get the information when we set up camp there. Your mission will be difficult. We need to get this information after twenty-five days, while avoiding capture by Jabal's followers."*

"So you want us to travel what would usually take thirty days, observe Jabal's army, gather all the military information related to it, and accomplish all of that in less than twenty-five day?!" asked Fida, somewhat indignant.

The Khalifa responded, *"I trust you both. I do not know a deer that can climb or fence like you, Fida, nor do I know a raptor that can get into my court as Baz did, despite the increased number of guards that day. I need you both to use the same agility and speed*

---

[1] Al-Oyoon Al-Hamia—Translation: Hot springs.

to track the movements of those masses and return safe. You leave immediately. Your horses and equipment are ready."

The court was completely silent. I looked around, only to find my father's face beaming with pride, as a tear escaped from his eye. I moved toward him, kissed his forehead, and said, "I promise to bring you honor, Father."

"May Allah protect you, my son, and return you safe to us," my father replied.

I was about to step toward the court's door, but was surprised when my father pulled me by my arm and pulled me close to his chest, embracing me. He then pushed me away and looked into my eye with a deep, caring look before he waved to me to go.

◦✦✧✦✧✦✧✦✧✦◦

We barely made it to the edge of the Prince Ibn Obaid Allah forest before the last bit of sunlight vanished. We got off our horses to prepare to spend the dark night there after a long, hard day.

"We shall spend the night here, and tomorrow we shall look for Shaheen and Heraak.[1] I hope they will agree to join us on this mission, otherwise, we shall have to look for others, and we have no time to pass through the forests of the Dokhan[2] mountain to find

---

[1] Heraak—Translation: Movement.
[2] Dokhan—Translation: Smoke.

66

Hakoom or Awqab," said Fida, who was exhausted from the day's efforts.

"I know Shaheen well, and I am certain that he would never refuse me anything. As for Heraak, however, I have warned you many times of his moodiness."

Fida giggled as he said, "Aren't we all?"

I lit my lamp to inspect the area around us, while Fida laid our quilts after he had cleared the area from stones. I gathered some wood to start a fire to keep us warm.

"We shall not start any fires during this mission," he said firmly.

"But we need it to stay warm," I cautioned him.

"Use more quilts, if you need to, but I will not freely inform our enemies of our location or our movements. This mission is extremely secretive and important."

"May Allah give me strength to overcome the hardship of traveling with you," I said, with utter disapproval, but Fida ignored my tone.

"Do you really think we will find that Jabal actually gathered an army to fight the Khalifa?"

"We all know that Jabal has always dreamt of authority and power, but we never imagined that he would dare challenge the Khalifa publicly. What puzzles me is how he convinced other Yaqteenyans to follow him."

"Baz, faith in the unknown is not an easy thing. We, as humans, always search instinctively for the logic and evidence that support what we are doing. Jabal has taken advantage of that to call to question what the Moors have passed on to you. When trust is gone, manipulating the masses becomes easy, and to be honest, I hold my father and the rest of the Moors partially responsible. Your question the day my father gathered us in his court was logical and important. My father not answering it truthfully, as well as his insistence—along with the rest of his advisors—in denying anyone from crossing the Okeanós, to bring us back evidence of the truth about all that was passed on to us regarding the history of Islam and Al-Andalus, will be our downfall. What I fear the most is that our fathers' sins have followed us here and what happened in Al-Andalus will repeat itself, causing the genocide of all who disagree with Jabal."

I looked at him with my mouth opened wide, astonished by his words. I thought all Moors were unanimous regarding the upholding of the isolation law, and that it was not debatable, but for one of them to utter a word of objection to it, especially when that someone is the son of the Khalifa himself, the thought of this happening would have never crossed my mind for a second.

"You seem surprised. Is that not what you believe? So why the surprise?"

"But you are a Moor, and not just any Moor. You are the Khalifa's only son, and the future Khalifa, after your father's long life, so how could *you say such a thing?"*

"What does that have to do with thinking for myself? Or are you implying that Moors do not have the brains to think, especially the blood line of the Khalifa?"

I started to sweat, so I replied, nervously. "No. God forbid. That was not what I meant. What I meant was…"

"No worries, Baz. I know exactly what you meant, but what sort of Khalifa would I be if I did not think for myself?! Yes, there was a need, at that time, to impose the isolation law, as Muslims were weak and our relationship with the Yaqteenyans was weaker. We were immigrants fleeing in order to protect our religion, wealth, honor, and science. We arrived in a strange land where we had no home or friends, but today, we are strong amongst brothers who love us as much as we love them. So, why the fear, and why the insistence on a law that was passed a few years short of three centuries ago, when times and places have changed, as did the reason for which that law was created?"

"So why didn't you say something? Why haven't you tried to convince your father to send an expedition across the Okeanós and return with proof?"

"I do not dare oppose my father in public. I had debated this with him in private more than once since this conflict began, but he wouldn't listen to me. In fact, he keeps saying that this was your influence on me, and that if I thought about it independently,

away from your friendship, I would not have come to the conclusion I came to."

"My friendship? But we have never talked about this before. I was careful not to get into this debate with you to protect our friendship. If your father was against this friendship, and, specifically, its influence over your logic, why did he send you with me on a mission that would provide me with twenty-five days in which to influence you even more?"

"I think he thought that my interaction with you on a mission like this would make me understand why we have to maintain the isolation law, but in my opinion, the real reason we are maintaining the isolation law is our fear of the results of that first expedition."

"What do you mean?"

"I think that the Moors have lost their faith in what they said long before the Yaqteenyans did, so they fear that first expedition because it was the true test of what they believe in. If the expedition results in anything contrary to what we have been saying, it would be the end of what we have built here, and the end of the brotherhood that unites us."

The forest regained its silence. I laid my head on the ground as I looked into the heavens, where the stars were scattered with such clarity that I almost felt I could pluck them right out of the sky. I broke the silence and spoke. "If you have lost your faith in what you have delivered to us, I still have faith in

70

everything you brought us." I did not get a response from Fida. He must have fallen asleep from exhaustion.

Yasser Bahjatt ياسر بهجت

(5)

Stranger

Yasser Bahjatt ياسر بهجت

A Friday of Jumad the former 291 FG

I spent the last four days in Akadeer, staking out the marid's house, where he was holding the Yaqteenyan old man. I got to know this huge city after I rented a room from the marid's back side neighbor. It seemed that this city was one of the most important cities of this sector, as people from all over passed through it for trade, or to search for a job within the many blessings that Allah had bestowed upon the city. On the west side of the city and covering almost a third of its waterfront was its harbor that was bursting with life day and night. Military and trade ships of all shapes and sizes occupied the harbor and the city depended on the passengers' spending, whether it was to buy products, enjoy its immense variety of food, or stay in its hostels. In addition, the city hosts a lot of fishing boats that supply the city with huge amounts of fish and whales that are lined up on the edges of the harbor for sale. I have never seen a harbor of this size or this many ships in one place. The ships within the city walls filling the horizon seemed like locusts. Amongst them today was a ship the likes of which I had not seen before. Its mast could almost touch the clouds. On its sides were hundreds of cannons. I heard

the harbor workers whisper its name, Al-Anqaa.[1]
They say that its captain is Ameer Al-Bahr[2], the
greatest commander in the Ottoman navy Orhan
Basha Reis, and that he was there to celebrate the
anniversary of the conquest of Rome (I think I have
heard of this city before, but I can't remember where).
The city's walls extend a few thousand feet into the
Okeanós. It ends with a tower on both sides. Every
tower had two platforms. The first was the same
height as the city walls, and the second was fifty arms
above it. Giant cannons poked out of them that I
could clearly see from that distance. A few iron chains
extended between the two towers, making them an
impenetrable barrier, blocking any ship from entering
the city limits. As for the city's center, there you
would find spacious gardens filled with fruitful trees
and aromatic flowers, where children would play and
lovers would stroll, surrounded by well-placed polls
with hanging lanterns that were lit after sunset for a
few hours, giving strollers and visitors a chance to
relax there after a long day, without fear of darkness.
Beyond that, houses and buildings were intertwined
and alleys branched out between them. What was also
strange was the fact that this city was occupied and
visited by a lot of dark-skinned marids. It seemed that
this city was a gateway between the two worlds of

---

[1] Al-Anqaa—Translation: The Phoenix.
[2] Ameer Al-Bahr—Translation: Is the title of the head of the navy.
Translated to Prince of the Sea, it is thought to be the origin for the
word Admiral.

Jinn and Humans, and that everyone there got used
to their existence, for I had not noticed that anyone
was afraid of them or their existence amongst them.
Particularly strange, however, was the fact that
mosques were scattered in every corner of the city,
mosques of every size and building style. Its minarets
raised the sounds of Athan and mixed the voices of
muezzins into one voice that echoed throughout the
city. How was this possible? This contradicted
everything I was taught since childhood, that Islam
was eradicated in the old world when Granada fell,
that the Moors were the last surviving Muslims, and
they had fled for their faith to Yaqteenya. Did others
survive, flee to this land, and rebuild Islam there, that
close to their enemies?! That was the most logical
explanation for the existence of this city, its walls and
military harbor, and its residents' clothing that
resembled the traditional Moors' clothing, which
made my Yaqteenyan clothing that had a fusion of
leather and cloth strange and stand out, even though
the city was used to strangers and passersby, and did
not pay them much attention. I had to buy their cloth
garments from one of the merchants to blend in. I also
had to break into a smeltery on the edges of the city
one night to wipe Yaqteenya's writings off my
dirhams and dinars to make them more acceptable to
the merchants. I tried to avoid interacting with people
as much as possible, to avoid raising any suspensions,
especially among soldiers who were looking for me.
That was the main reason I did not pray in any of

77

their mosques during those days, for fear of being found out.

After four days in Akadeer, the marid came out of his house after the mosques had called for prayer, but this call was not at its usual time. It was a decent period prior to the Thuhur prayer time. It must have been Friday, and this was the first call. I followed our friend until he arrived at one of the mosques, where he took off his shoes and went inside. I followed him inside, but lost him in the crowd. I had to sit amongst the worshipers because if I left then, it would no doubt raise their suspicions. My eyes sifted through the worshipers in hopes of finding the marid, but there were too many worshipers, mostly marids, making my task nearly impossible. I do not know how much time had passed before the Imam stepped up to the platform and greeted us. The muezzin followed him with the call to prayer. I, unfortunately, did not listen much to his preaching, as I was busy looking for the marid, in addition to my fear of being found out. All I remember of his preaching was the Imam's extended talk about how important that day was, and how Allah had blessed them with the conquering of Rome by the hands of the hero Ameer Al-Bahr, Hayreddin Barbarossa, less than a century after the conquering of Constantinople by the hands of Mehmed the Conqueror, and that the conquering of Rome was like a consolation to the Islamic nation for the fall of Granada before that conquering by almost *half a century. That did not sound logical to me. How did the Moors conquer Constantinople with all of its mighty fortifications, only to reach the end of their civilization and the fleeing of their homes only fifty years later? And the Imam did not talk of the fall of Granada as a crossroad between existence and obliteration, as we were taught in Yaqteenya. Rather he talked of it as a lost battle followed by a sequence of victories. Additionally, the Imam did not mention the Moors in his speech, nor did he talk of their suffering after the fall of Granada, nor the struggle to rebuild what they had lost to the point that they could conquer Rome. All he spoke about were the Turkish generals or the Ottoman Sultans. All of these questions echoed through my head and distracted me from what was going on around me. I was surprised when one of the worshipers poked me. I just then noticed that he was standing there, as the muezzin called for the prayer to start. I stood in line with the rest of the worshipers, was about to put my hands on my right shoulder and left side of my waist to grip my sword and dagger, as I did my entire life, but I realized that all the other worshipers had their arms fall next to their sides, so I did the same, out of fear of standing out as a stranger amongst them. But how were they praying in this strange position that I had never seen or heard of before? And what was the status of my prayer, now that I had adopted the same position? Should I redo my prayer when I get back to my room? Oh, have mercy on me, dear God, my*

79

attendance at this prayer had only added to my confusion that started the moment I began this trek to understand the Moors' history. Every time I tried to answer one question, I faced another that was more confusing than its predecessor.

The prayer was over and worshipers spread out in every direction, as I sat in my place trying to find the marid whom I followed into the mosque. Then suddenly, without warning, I found him, as he moved toward me, and our eyes met. I saw surprise in his black facial expression. He started to push worshipers in every direction so that he could get to me. He knew who I was. I had to escape before he caught up with me. The next moment, a worshiper crossed between us, blocking me out of his sight. I seized the moment and lost him amongst the remaining worshipers, and fled into the alley before he could find any trace of me.

◊⬡⬡⬡⬡⬡⬡⬡◊

I got back to my room, where I had set up a system that would allow me to listen to most of what was said in the marid's house. I fixed a bunch of probes into my room's wall that was next to his house, then connected them with thin threads to a piece of wood that would transfer the echo's movements to the echo enhancer that I had constructed from a leather piece stretched over a wooden frame. I had connected the enhancer to the

Hakee[1], to save the echoes that reached it if I were out of my room so that I could review them later. But the Hakee did not record any important conversations in the last several days. The old man did not wake until the moment I left that morning, as he was still feverish and exhausted from battling the Okeanós.

I stood in front of the enhancer, waiting to hear the marid's echo. I almost lost my balance when I heard the echo of his house's door slam shut, followed by the echo of the marid yelling, obviously nervous, "Himr, Himr, he is here!"

The marid did not get any response as he climbed the house's steps with extreme speed, until he stopped. I heard his voice yell, "Get up, Himr! We have no time! He is here!"

I heard incomprehensible mumbling, followed by the marid's angry voice. "Who else? Al-Baz, I knew that the soldiers were looking for one of you, but I thought it was one of the sailors. I did not expect Baz to survive drowning. I did not expect that anyone could enter the city with all of the soldiers looking for him. Do you know what this means? Baz's arrival here means that our mission is now even more complicated."

I heard a husky voice that I thought was the old

---

[1] Hakee—Translation: This is a play on words. The word could be a derivation from Hekayah, which means story. It would then mean the story teller, or, from Heyakah, which means knitting, so it would then mean the knitter.

man's: "That's Khidr's[1] opinion, so why does he not come here to fix it himself?"

"You know the rules of the covenant well enough to know that we are not allowed to operate outside our zones unless the change has affected our zone, and to this moment, the change in his zone is almost nonexistent."

"And who said that this change was not to the right path? Don't you see what a blessing we have here?"

"It is not you who decides what the right path is. We have discussed this, and the rest of the covenant has agreed that this path must be fixed. Is this why Baz got here? Are you trying to maintain this path?"

"I did what I was asked. It is not my fault that he has made it here."

"This discussion is futile. We must find him and stop him before things get worse. We must inform Bayad[2] of what is going on here. I suspect Baz will travel to his zone."

I then heard some harmonized sounds, like a thousand bees moving in the old man's room. The sound lasted for a few moments, and then stopped as suddenly as it started.

"We must move now. We must find Al-Baz before the soldiers do."

---

[1] Khidr—Translation: Comes from the word Akhdar, meaning green, loosely translated to greenish.

[2] Bayad—Translation: Comes from the word Abyad, meaning white, loosely translated to whitish.

It sounds like the marid was helping the old man stand and lean on him, as they went down the stairs until they reached the stable. He then helped him ride a horse to leave the house in a hurry.

That day kept increasing my confusion with every passing moment, and the day was still young, but I now knew that Himr was working with this marid. I believed that he had something to do with the sinking of my ship, and that they wanted to stop me from completing my mission. Were they upholding the isolation law? What bad luck I had. I was now wanted by the soldiers of this city, and by this covenant that they spoke of. I had to get out of the city to complete my mission. I had lost precious time there. Dear lord, what surprises awaited me that day!

❖◇❖◇❖◇❖◇❖

The military had full control over all the gates in and out of this city. No one could get in or out without showing their valid credentials. As for the Okeanós' side, its walls extended quite far into it, making swimming out of the city nearly impossible, especially while carrying all the stuff that I had gathered from my ship's wreckage. The only way out now was for me to sneak onto a ship that was leaving. I tried getting a map to understand the area and chose my next destination, but I could not find anyone who would sell me navigational maps. I did, however, find a sailor who agreed to draw me the general outlines of this country for a dirham. Akadeer was part of what he called the Ottoman Khalifa. It was in the far west of this nation, in what he called Africa, and below that was Jabal Tariq's strait, what the sailor called the land of the Spaniards. It was part of a land mass he called Europe. He assured me that it was what used to be called Al-Andalus. To the left of that was the northern coast of Africa, facing the upper coast of Europe. He said that the majority of it was either under the direct Ottoman rule, such as Rome, or under the rule of some European kings who paid tribute to the Ottomans, such as the French. To the left of that was Egypt, which had the Pharaohs' pyramids. To its left was the Arabian Peninsula, where Makkah and Madina were. Below that was Al-Sham, and below it was the land of the Turks, where the capital of the Ottomans was Istanbul, where Europe meets what he called Asia. This was going to be my route. I would document my trip in full until I performed Haj, so that I would be the first Yaqteenyan to ever circle the Kabaa.

My best option then was the Al-Anqaa. I knew that it was going to sail toward Rome at dawn, to arrive there some fifty days later, and, as per the sailor's information, all ships sailing east must stop at least for one night in Sibtah's harbor on Jabal Tariq's strait. That would be my first stop, where I would find a way to go to Al-Andalus from there.

I headed to the harbor, where Al-Anqaa was

anchored. I stood fascinated by its size, and the moonlight reflected off the surface of the Okeanós increased its prestige, while the lights from the lanterns increased its mystery. I could not help myself. I pulled out Saed Al-Zilal[1], and captured Al-Anqaa's shadows, and behind it were the city walls extended into the Okeanós. Some time passed and dawn was almost upon us. I watched the ship in hopes of finding a way to reach it. It was under heavy guard and only those authorized to do so could get near it. I then heard Antarah's voice: "I know that I am not a passenger of this ship. Do you know who I am? I am Agha Antarah."

"Sir, I know very well who you are, but my orders were clear, not to allow anyone near the ship, let alone onto it without the direct approval of Ameer Al-Bahr."

"Then send for him at once," Antarah said.

The soldier looked baffled as he said, "Send for him? Me? Sorry, Sir, but you well know that I cannot do that. I am but a simple soldier and do not dare send for Ameer Al-Bahr. He sends for me, not the other way around."

"I have no time for this nonsense. I must get to Istanbul fast, and this is the fastest ship that can get me there. I must speak to the Sultan in person," Antarah said.

"I can only allow you to go accompanied by one

---

[1] Saed Al-Zilal—Translated: Shadow Hunter.

85

of my soldiers. That is the best I can do, and I hope that you will not make me regret this."

"Very well. I will go talk to him and come back with his approval to board the ship, along with my company," Antarah replied.

I was observing this chatter from a few feet away. I noticed Hamzah standing by Antarah, and next to him was that beauty. I could not believe that Antarah was her father. How could a marid father such a lovely, beautiful girl?! Behind them were a few soldiers in a different uniform than the one worn by the sailors. They had a few horses and two camels loaded with luggage. I noticed one of the soldiers moving slowly away from the group. He then went to one of the merchants scattered around the harbor and started to browse through his merchandise. That was my chance.

I moved toward the soldier while I carried my bundle over my shoulder. I pretended to bump into him by mistake. He got really angry, but controlled himself, for fear of being busted for leaving his post without his captain's approval. I pretended to apologize. As I leaned on his shoulder, I jabbed his nick with a strong sedative, and within a few seconds, he started to lose his balance. I helped him stand, leading him away from his group without any resistance. I got behind a bunch of boxes piled on the docks. The soldier had totally lost consciousness. I removed his military armor, put it on myself, and *found a few identification documents inside. I returned to his post next to the camels and placed my bundle on its back. I pretended to inspect everyone passing by us, to avoid the rest of the soldiers' eyes, especially those of Hamzah and Antarah's daughter.*

I heard the call for Fajur prayer, and with it, Antarah appeared to be walking back toward us, and with him was the soldier who had accompanied him.

"Ameer Al-Bahr has granted them permission to board Al-Anqaa and accompany us. Let them in quickly, as he wants to sail at once."

I stepped forward with them, protecting the convoy's back. None of them realized what had happened. We boarded Al-Anqaa, and one of the ship's sailors pointed me toward the ship's stables to take the camels and horses there, allowing me to move away from Antarah and to take back my bundle, as I disappeared on the ship until we arrived at Sibtah.

Yasser Bahjatt ياسر بهجت

(6)
Shaheen

Yasser Bahjatt ياسر بهجت

Tuesday night the fourteenth of Ramadan 287 FG

Fida and I snuck out of Qurtuba's mosque during taraweeh prayers, after I was certain that my father had moved up a few rows, and that he was not going to realize we were skipping prayers. The full moon lit up the night sky. There were many worshipers that night, which made our escape from the mosque unnoticed much harder than we expected. We arrived at one of the ten external mosque gates. I am still amazed at its size and towering height, which almost touched the mosque's second-story roof. Each gate was at least eight arms high. I came back to reality when Fida poked me between my ribs, as he pointed toward one of the gate's sides, where a soldier from the royal guards was standing, while observing activities outside the mosque. That was what I had feared. The guards knew Fida well, and some knew me, too. None of them would allow Fida out of the mosque without an escort, which meant that word of our sneaking out would reach the Khalifa, and then my father, and neither of us would survive that. Fida whispered into my ear, "Let's climb the gates to the second story and exit through the stairs there."

I passed my eyes over the gate from bottom to top, then back to its bottom again. What madness this was! But we had no choice. I swallowed hard and shook my head in agreement. Fida stepped toward the gate and started climbing. I followed him. The Imam rose from kneeling during the first set. We had to reach the second floor before he was done with this set, otherwise it would be our end. Fida reached the second floor after the worshipers had knelt and I was on his tail. Fida inspected the space between him and the fence that surrounded the second floor. Without any warning, Fida pushed his body with all his strength toward the fence and jumped, slamming into it. He held on to its edge. I breathed a sigh of relief as I climbed another step and watched Fida trying to lift himself over the fence. My right hand moved swiftly, extending toward the fence while I moved my left hand to hold onto the edge of the gate without thinking, so that when Fida's grip slipped from the fence, I caught his left hand in the last moment. He screamed in terror and pain, as he looked into my eyes with gratitude.

"You two, what are you doing there?" asked the guard, who was now standing directly beneath us. He must have heard Fida's scream.

"We're busted. I'll swing and throw you over there," I said to Fida. He shook his head in understanding, and started to move his body with my body's swings while the soldier watched us. I let go of Fida as I raised him with all my might, tossing him through the air. He fell into the second floor of the mosque, then stood up and dangled his body over the *fence. I jumped toward him, and he caught me and helped me over the fence.*

"Stop where you are!" yelled the soldier.

"We must escape before he catches us," said Fida, as he ran with all the speed he could muster toward the steps, climbing down them in the blink of an eye. I followed him step by step, and when we were ten feet away from the mosque, we heard the soldier calling from behind us. That added to our excitement and speed, until we reached the city limits. We disappeared into the crowds and moved toward the forest, leaving the city and its walls behind us.

✦❖❖❖❖❖❖✦

We thought it would be a great idea to get out to the woods that night. We believed that we could easily hunt in the middle of the night, especially with the moonlight shining like it was. We thought that hunting deer and other critters would be much easier while they were asleep. And on that particular day, we were going to become men after the first full moon after our two-hundredth had shone upon us. The next day, after Iftar,[1] we would both know our totem, and I would get my name that I would live with for the rest of my life that God had written for me to live. That might be the last night I would be called by the name that I had known for the past two-hundred

---

[1] Iftar—Translation: Is the first meal you eat. In Ramadan, that would be at sunset, which is why it is called breakfast, to break your fast.

months. I would not hear anyone call me Robaa after that day. Oh, how I hated the name that my elder brother tagged me with to signify that I was the fourth of my siblings. But what would my name be?

"Fida, what name do you think you will be given tomorrow?"

"I am not worried about that. Since the foundation of the Yaqteenyan nation, none of the Khalifas' sons has ever had his name changed," he replied.

"That is not true. What about the Khalifa Raad Al-Samaa[1]?" I asked.

"That was the first Khalifa of the Yaqteenyan nation, and his name was changed after he reached forty, after the battle of the hot springs. That name change was a show of respect by the Yaqteenyans to the Moorish Khalifa, and his acceptance of the name was a show of respect of Yaqteenyan traditions, but it has never happened since," Fida replied.

"You might be next! Yet you participate in the night of the full moon to specify your childrens' totems."

"I see you are very excited about this month's activities, Robaa," Fida said to me.

"My patience is worn out waiting for this day. What name do you think they will cast on me? Fearsome Monster, Mighty Dragon, Burning Sky?"

"Hahaha, say Flipping Monkey, or Hanging

---

[1] Raad Al-Samaa—Translation: Sky Thunder.

Spider, or Jumping Cricket."

"Laugh as much as you want. I am sure I will receive a great name, an even greater totem, and I will ..."

"Hush!" Fida pointed toward a bunch of entangled trees. I listened and heard the sound of movement behind them. Fida raised his bow, pointing his arrow toward the trees, while I took out my dagger fitted with a pistol and pointed it in the same direction. A moving shadow appeared. Fida sent his arrow toward the shadow, and the forest trembled with the sound of a monster howling. I released what was in my pistol's guts and the explosion echoed along with the flash of flame. Its orange hue reflected off our surroundings, making the forest more terrifying than it was in the moonlight. The shadow moved toward us with astonishing speed. It was but a few steps away from Fida when it stood on its feet. It was a bear more than five arms high, grinning with his white fangs that glimmered in the moonlight as he swung his claws with anger. Frightened, Fida carefully moved backward. His foot hit a log as he fell on his back. I froze in place for a moment while the bear looked at me with fiery-red eyes, then returned his gaze toward Fida. As the bear stepped toward him, Fida tried to move away from him, but he couldn't move. The bear got close to Fida and was about to unleash one of his claws at him when, without thinking, I attacked the bear. He slammed my chest hard with the back of his right paw, throwing me a few feet into the air before I slammed into a tree trunk, causing extreme pain in my back. I saw something fall out of the tree, right in front of me. I could not make out what it was. I tried to stand up to defend Fida, whom the bear had resumed moving toward, but my pain limited my movement. The bear fell toward Fida, ferociously waving his claw at him, so Fida quickly moved out of its way. The bear's claw hit the ground with such force that sand and debris flew everywhere. The bear grew angrier, so he raised his other claw to slam it into Fida. Out of the trees came a giant moose, running at full speed, slamming his horns into the bear and throwing him away from Fida. The bear stood on his four legs and growled, then sprinted toward the moose to engage in a fight, the likes of which I had never seen. The bear's sharp claws and the moose's wide horns! The fight ended when the moose swiftly attacked the bear's head. The bear then slapped the moose in its head, with his claw completely tearing the moose apart and forcing it to fall with all of its weight on Fida, but the moose had also struck the bear on the side of its head. The bear's slap smashed the moose's horns into the bear's head, causing the bear to stumble backward and fall dead next to Fida. I tried to stand up once more, but I lost consciousness first.

❖❖❖❖❖❖❖❖❖❖

For a moment, I thought I was in my room, with

my sister Nasmat Al-Rabee[1] opening my window, as usual, and spreading the curtains so that the sunlight would shatter my sleep. I put my arms over my eyes to block the sunlight, as I said, annoyed, "Nasma! Can't you stop, even for one day?"

I suddenly woke and cut myself off. I remembered that I was in the forest. That must've been a dream. My entire body ached, especially my back and head. I slowly opened my eyes. At first I could not see anything, between the blinding sunlight and the dizziness caused by my head slamming into the tree trunk the day before after that bear tossed me.

"Fida!" I yelled, when I recalled what had happened. I rubbed my eyes, trying to force them to see, and I panicked when the first thing I saw was the pool of blood surrounding Fida and his body lying underneath that moose. I forced myself up and moved toward him carefully. I felt his neck to feel for his carotid arterial pulse. Thank God he was still alive! "Fida! Fida!" I kept repeating, as I shook him until he woke up.

"Robaa?! How did you get… where am I? I can't move!"

"I will try to raise this moose off of you, while you try to slip from underneath him."

I shoved my arms under the moose and started grunting as I tried with all my strength to raise it off of Fida. The moose rose a bit and Fida started to move

---

[1] Nasmat Al-Rabee—Translation: Spring breeze.

97

out from underneath him, but I slipped, allowing the moose's body to once again fall on Fida's legs, causing him to scream in pain.

"Aaaarrre you ok?! Answer me!" I yelled at Fida.

"What do you think? Do I look OK?" he answered, sarcastically.

"Today we will become men. Bruises do not bother us. I meant, 'do you have any broken bones or are you bleeding'?"

"What nonsense is this? BRUISES?! I spent the night pinned under a dead moose's body, in a pool of blood. I think it's the moose's blood mixed with the bear's blood, so no, I'm not bleeding. And no, I don't think I have any broken bones, either," Fida said, somewhat indignant.

"Then you must carry on and ignore the pain," I said. "I will get you out of there."

"How about we continue this inspiring conversation after I get out from underneath this dead moose?" Fida asked, again sarcastically.

I gave him a sideways look and furiously glanced at him, as I once again raised the moose off of Fida, allowing him to escape from underneath him this time. Fida then felt his head, where I could see some dried blood.

Fida angrily complained, "That reckless moose caused me to hit my head on that rock!"

"That moose saved us, and gave his life doing so. Had it not been for Allah's mercy and that moose *intervening, that bear would have ripped us both to shreds, so have some respect for the moose!"*

"But why?" asked Fida, as he inspected the bear's body where he had struck him with his arrow before I froze in his place as he pointed toward the trees, where he heard sounds of movement. I tried to pull my dagger from its place, but recalled that I had lost it the day before when the bear had struck me. I looked around for it, only to find a falcon chick squirming on the ground. I thought it was what had fallen out of the tree the night before. I had no time to deal with the chick just then, as I needed to find my dagger. I used my hands to search the pool of blood, while Fida slowly moved toward the trees and I was trying to convince him not to, for fear of it being a second bear.

"It's a baby moose," Fida said joyously when he crossed the tree branches and disappeared from my sight.

"I think his father attacked the bear to protect him," Fida conjectured.

"I don't think so. He could have just fled with his kid and left us to our fate with the bear. We are to blame for what happened to his father and to this chick. We must take them with us to Qurtuba and take care of them," I said.

"Take care of them? Where? In the Palace?! I think that hit on your head was much harder than the one on mine," Fida said.

"And, in your humble opinion, what is the

alternative?" I asked, again sarcastically.

"Alternative? They are jungle animals. Therefore, the alternative is to leave them where they are and return quickly, before our fathers kill us."

"I will not return without them. We caused this problem when we recklessly came into the forest, so the least we can do to show our gratitude is to take care of them until they grow up."

"Ok, OK, but we leave right away. My father must have sent his soldiers to look for me."

I approached the falcon chick to carry him. He kept hitting me with his beak and wings, but I carried him anyway, while the baby moose followed Fida, without Fida even telling him to. So, we were on our way back to the city.

◦✧✧✧✧✧✧✧✧◦

We arrived at the city gates and none of the soldiers noticed us, although they were nervously inspecting the faces of everyone in search of Fida. None of them even looked twice at the baby moose or asked any questions. I think the fact we were covered in mud and blood hid our true identities from them. Fida insisted that we pass by my house, to leave the animals there and to clean up before going to the palace, as his father would not be able to control himself if he saw him like that. We arrived at my family's barn without being noticed. We left the falcon chick and the moose there, and then we *continued around the house until we got to my room's shut window. I slipped my dagger between its flaps and smiled at Fida, as I gestured mockingly to him to enter as I raised my dagger to move the latch from its place and open the window. Fida's expression suddenly changed. I slowly turned my head toward the window, only to find my mother standing in the middle of my room, furious! "Where have you two been all night? The entire city is looking for you. Get in here, at once!" she yelled at us.*

I was about to jump through the window, into my room, but I stopped when I heard my mother's growl and saw her angry face. I gestured to Fida to go to the front door of the house. When we entered, my mother looked us both up and down, and then, in a caring voice, very different from the angry one she had greeted us with just moments ago, asked, "What happened to the two of you? What is all of this blood? Is either of you hurt?"

My mother inspected me as she passed her hand over my head before I groaned in pain when her hands reached the bruise at the back of my head, where I had slammed into the tree trunk. She held it together as she shifted her interest to Fida with inquisitive eyes.

Fida volunteered, "I do not think I have any injuries other than a bruise on the side of my head." He then pointed at the blood covering his clothes and explained very nonchalantly, "This is not our blood. It's the blood of a moose and a bear."

101

"Moose?! Bear?!"

"Long story. Can I please have a shower while Robaa explains? I do not wish for my father to see me like this."

She shook her head, understanding, and pointed toward the bathroom. She said to Fida, "Robaa will bring you some clean clothes. I think you are both almost the same size."

"Thank you, Aunty," Fida said to my mother.

He went off to bathe and left me to tell her what had happened to us the day before, as well as receive the full scolding alone.

◦⬦⬦⬦⬦⬦⬦⬦◦

Even though Fida insisted that I accompany him to the palace, I refused, as I had already had enough scolding to sustain me for a few decades, and I did not think I could take more scolding from the Khalifa directly. My mother insisted that I shower before she and I took care of the two animals I left in the barn, so that the moose would not smell his father's blood on my clothes. Even though she had scolded me harshly for what I had done the day before, she defended me when my father returned, furious over what I had done. He had heard everything from Fida in the Khalifa's court. My mother told my father that my concern for the two orphaned animals and insistence on not leaving them in the forest was proof that I cared for the safety of all of Allah's creatures, as well as the recognition of gratitude toward every creature, those were characters of righteous men.

Mother spent the rest of the day with me, preparing me for that night's ceremony, telling me to dress in my best outfit and to spray my sweetest scent. She told me the stories of my ancestors and their relationship with Allah's creatures on this earth, and how that relationship had changed to a deeper understanding and stronger relationship after the Moors came to us. The Holy Quran and the hadeeth[1] that they had brought with them had interpretations of life and spirits that were much deeper than what my ancestors thought. She then told me the stories of creatures told in the Quran, starting with Solomon's hoopoe, then ants, bees, and cattle, and ending with the spider. Then she talked about creatures in the hadeeth from the camel of Prophet Mohammad— peace be upon him—and how it chose the location for his mosque. She also told the story of his palm's trunk that he used to stand on top of while preaching, and the love relationship between the prophet—peace be upon him—and Uhud mountain. Although I had heard those stories hundreds of times, it was the first time I listened without interrupting her. This time, my mother was talking to me alone, caring for only me, proud of only me. I had never felt that way before. I do not recall spending a full day with her alone before. She was always busy with Father and

---

[1] Hadeeth are the stories and sayings of the prophet Mohammad. Peace be upon him.

my siblings, and the house, or the Khalifa's wife and matters of state. I wished that day would last forever. I wished I could remain her only concern, but, as the poet said, "Everything once whole must start its diminution." It was now just before sunset, so we all went out to Qurtuba's main square, where all ceremonies and celebrations take place, but that day, it was filled with delegations from every corner of Yaqteenya. That night was special because, first, it was the mid of Ramadan, which meant that at sunset, we would celebrate with an Iftar to thank Allah for blessing us with its fasting, and second, it was the Khalifa's only son's totem ceremony, which meant the Khalifa himself would attend.

Lanterns were scattered all over the square, making its light out-shine the setting sun. Tents were set up all over the square with assortments of delights, and in its center, a stage was set, where all the clans' wise men sat, including my father. Next to him was the wise man of Qurtuba. At one corner stood the totems' masters greeting new delegations of youth to teach us and train us about our totems that we would find out that night. Despite all the hustle and bustle that engulfed the square, all eyes turned toward me and my mother because of her insistence that I take the moose and falcon chick with me to that night's ceremony, and that I should go to Qurtuba's wise man the moment I arrived to the square and tell him what had happened to us the night before, as he was in charge of that night's ceremonies, and that these events might affect it. I did not understand what she meant by that last comment, but I was not about to refuse her request, no matter how much embarrassment it might cause me in front of all of those crowds.

I arrived at the stage in the center of the square and noticed my father looking at me in astonishment, as he nodded toward the moose and falcon chick on his back. I ignored his looks and gestures as I looked at Qurtuba's wise man, who said, "Al-salmu alikum,[1] wise man of Qurtuba."

"Al-salmu alikum wa rahmato Allah wa barakatuh[2] Robaa, who are your friends?"

"They have a story. Would you agree to inspect them as I tell it to you?" I asked.

"Certainly, Son."

The wise man stepped off the stage and came close to the moose and placed his hand on its head, petting it with compassion. He then said, "Let us walk as you tell me their story."

We circled the square as I told him about what happened the previous night, while he shook his head and made mumbling sounds every now and then. I felt he was absent-minded, as if he was not really listening to me, that he was just being nice to me. Well, no more. When I was done with my story, the wise man stopped the moose and stood directly in

---

[1] Peace be upon you.
[2] May peace and Allah's blessings and mercy be upon you.

front of him and looked into his eyes, then started making strange sounds, to which the moose responded with similar sounds. That went on for a few moments, and then the wise man looked at me and said, "He says his father stepped in to save Fida by command of Khumas Al-Ahmar. Did you meet him?"

"Khumas? Al-Ahmar? Is he the fifth of his siblings, as I am the fourth of mine?"

"Something of that sort. He is the fifth of his group. As far as I know, some call them Himr. They are but a legend, but this moose is totally convinced that his father met this Al-Ahmar, and that he commanded him to save Fida. If that was true, it changes a lot of things."

"Changes what? And what significance is this Al-Ahmar?"

"Do not concern yourself with such things, my son. Go back and mingle with the rest of the young men in the square and leave these two with me."

I returned, but the wise man had filled my head with confusion. Who was this Al-Ahmar? And why did he command the moose to save Fida? In fact, why did he not save himself? I sat at one of the tables awaiting Athan. I was starving. I had not eaten anything since the previous day's Iftar. I saw the wise man return to the stage with the two animals, which he handed over to one of his assistants, who took them backstage. A few moments later, the Khalifa showed up, followed by his wives and Fida, who separated *from them and came toward me when he saw me, to sit with me while his father went to sit on stage with the wise men. Then Athan echoed in the square and everyone's attention was on Iftar. We then lined up to pray Maghrib before the ceremonies started.*

◦✧✦✧✦✧✦✧✦◦

The chatter slowly settled in the square, as all eyes focused on Qurtuba's wise man, who stood at the center of the stage.

"On this blessed night and the second third of this holy month, a group of our sons and daughters will become men and women. Today, each of them will know their relationship with the rest of Allah's creatures through knowing his totem, allowing each of them to know the depth of our relationship with this vast universe. Most of them will receive tonight the names they live by for the rest of their lives, so that this connection will stay with them for as long as Allah gives them this life." He then signaled to his assistants, who then disappeared backstage and returned with the moose and falcon chick. The sounds of the crowd's mumbling rose the moment they took the stage, while Fida looked at me with questioning eyes.

"I know this is not how we normally do things, but it seems that this night is much more special than we thought. The process of discovering one's totem takes a lot of effort and deep soul searching, assisted

by one of our wise men to decipher its code. On rare occasions, however, that happen every thousand months or so, a totem would choose its receptor, and on this night, I was surprised to know that we are about to meet two such young men at the same time. Let them both step up on stage so that we can start our ceremonies, while the rest of you come toward the stage as each group with one of our wise men. As for our young ladies, they will find special tents set up for them on the sides of the square to meet with our wise women, who shall help them. Robaa, son of Al-Thib Al-Hakeem, come to the stage, along with Fida, son of our Khalifa."

I did not expect this. I was hoping to discover my totem in private, like everyone else does. I never knew that my totem discovery could happen in public. We moved with heavy steps toward the stage, as all eyes focused on us, awaiting our arrival to the stage. As their minds filled with curiosity and the desire to know the details, we went up the stage steps and Fida stood next to the wise man, and I next to him.

"This moose's father gave his life to save yours, for his conviction that the responsibility of saving this religion and this nation will someday fall onto your shoulders. The deer totem has chosen you. You move fast over solid grounds, you have the ability to change your direction with speed and agility; you must seek wisdom, for speed without wisdom will lead you and those you love toward destruction. You shall be known

108

from this day forward as Fida Al-Deen."

He then looked at me and said, "As for you, you have been selected by the raptor totem. You have far sight for truth, and move swiftly toward it before others even notice it. You are the best guide for your deer brother. We shall all know you from now on as Al-Baz Al-Monqad."

He then asked his assistants to bring the moose and falcon chick closer. Then he spoke again. "As for these two, they are your brothers from the forest. This moose's name is Heraak. As for the falcon, I was told by my raptor master friend that his name was Shaheen. They are from this day in your care until they grow up and can safely return to the forest. The masters of raptor and deer have insisted on personally teaching you the skills of your totems."

I neither cared nor noticed very much of what happened next that night. All I cared about was that I was no longer Robaa. I was now Al-Baz Al-Monqad, son of Al-Thib Al-Hakeem. Yes, that is now my name, my identity.

Yasser Bahjatt ياسر بهجت

(7)

A Mountain's

Legend

ياسر بهجت Yasser Bahjatt

The dawn of a Thursday in the final days of Jumad the former 291 FG

I spent five days and nights on Al-Anqaa's ship, pretending to be one of the soldiers of the Ottoman army. I avoided interacting with the ship's passengers as much as possible, for fear of my slang giving me away, as I had also noticed that some soldiers were talking in a language other than Arabic. It would make my situation much worse if any of them addressed me in that language. More importantly, I was avoiding Antarah, his daughter, and Hamzah. Only they could know how I looked. All of that forced me to stay awake most of the trip, as there was no place I could sleep without being noticed. That night, I dozed while sitting on the port side of the ship, leaning against its fence with my forehead, as I let my feet dangle to its side and wrapped myself in my cape that covered my head, as well. I woke up before the first sunlight. I felt a deep sadness when I awoke. I couldn't tell what it was at first, but, as time passed, I started to understand the feeling. It was sadness mixed with nostalgic longing over a few centuries of separation. I knew its source when the first lights of dawn showed me a mountain on the horizon, as if it was an island in that vast sea. I heard whispers carried by the wind of the name Jabal

113

Tariq. I hurried into the ship's hull to bring my saed, returned to where I was, and fixed the saed to the side of the ship as I tried to capture the shadows of this great mountain. I barely captured two shadows of the mountain before I froze when I heard a feminine voice standing next to me, saying, "Hide this tool immediately before my father can see it. He is following me here right now."

I did not dare to turn or ask any questions. I pulled the saed to hide it within my cape, then heard Antarah's voice behind me, saying, "There you are, Ablah. I see you are still infatuated by Jabal Tariq."

"I wish I could capture its shadows, as the author of this book claims, so that I could carry him with me everywhere."

Antarah giggled and replied, "This book you carry is but a fable of a mad man. Where does someone come up with a name such as Abed Rab Al-Shams Al-Aaqiby? Then claim to be able to capture the shadows that Allah had set free? Not only that, but that he could also trap sounds on a wooden rod knitted with a silk thread. What nonsense is this?!"

"But wouldn't that be wonderful?"

"Totally, as wonderful as if men could fly as Abbas wanted, and we all know what happened to him. He is now a lesson for every crazy dreamer."

"But, Father, those dreams are what propel us in life."

"Yes, they propel the youth. As for us, what

propels us is our dream that we would help you to one day come back to reality. As for now, I have an appointment with Ameer Al-Bahr to discuss the owner of this book. How are we to find a spy whose face we do not know? Do you not remember anything, my daughter?"

"It was a dark night. I only met him for a passing, frightening second.

"I wish I had paid more attention before we locked him up. None of my soldiers remembers his face, as his face was covered with sand when we found him, and my meeting with him in the cell was dark, and he was covering his face when he got to my office. That is why we must warn the Sultan and discuss our options with Ameer Al-Bahr. Very well. I will see you when we dock to disembark together." I heard his footsteps as he moved away and her as she moved closer to me. She stopped next to me and held onto the ship's side. I turned my face toward her with a puzzled look. I could not utter a single word. My facial expression slowly changed from puzzlement to fascination. I could not look away from her face, as I had never seen such beauty before and probably will never again. I do not know how to describe her. My linguistic capabilities do not do her justice. Her strange, dark skin that has no resemblance to any that I have seen in Yaqteenyans or Moors, and her green eyes as green as fields in spring. As for her body, I could talk for ages and not cover every detail. The wind has ensured exposing every minute detail of

115

her body and leaving absolutely nothing to the imagination. I suddenly was self-aware and became very shy. I said, "Sorry... I mean, thank you... I mean..."

"Calm down. I know who you are. You are that boy who escaped my father's grip about a month ago."

"Who? Me? Sorry, Miss, but what would a fugitive be doing riding a ship like this?!"

"Do not insult me. I knew who you were the moment I saw that saed in your hand, and now that I see the worry in your eyes, I am even more sure of it. You are the same person who left this book in my hands that day," and with that, she raised her left hand and waved the book at me. Then she continued, "If you deny it again, I will have to tell my father's guards to check you out for themselves."

"Let us assume, for the sake of argument, that I am who you claim I am. Why did you not inform them?"

"Two reasons. First—and more importantly—I need to make sure this is not just some fable, and second, I am sure you do not mean us any harm. If you did, you would have left my father in his office to burn, or harmed me that day to take this book from me, but such is not your character."

"And if I refuse?"

"You will have to explain what is in this book to my father's soldiers, and I assure you, they are very

116

slow learners."

I smiled. *"Hahaha. I think I would rather explain it to you, but your father?"*

"Do not worry. He is in a meeting with Ameer Al-Bahr, and will not finish their discussion before the ship docks in Sibtah's harbor."

"And what about after that?"

"We will cross that bridge when we come to it."

"Very well. How can I help you?"

She sat on the side of the ship and opened her book, as I sat next to her. I could still not believe that a marid like Antarah would father this creature, whose beauty overshadows all other women combined.

"Here, poisonous silver. What is that?!"

"This is a highly-poisonous material, but it reacts to light. It is dark, but changes, depending on the intensity of light to which it is exposed. If you expose it to direct sunlight, it loses color completely. We dissolve it in water along with some salts and acids, then we spray it on a piece of paper or cloth exposed to the lights reflected off of the object whose shadows we want to capture. The silver changes the color of the cloth, the water evaporates, and the salts and acids conserve the silver's color."

"But how do you capture the shadows of a mountain that is all of this distance away from here?"

"We use a scope connected to…"

I never expected to meet someone with such interest in these sciences in the old world, for

117

everything we were told about them hinted that they were not civilized, let alone that such a person would be so beautiful, and with such unique ability to comprehend such advanced concepts. Time passed quickly, only to be abruptly ended when we arrived at Sibtah's harbor.

"We have arrived at the harbor. My father will start looking for me now. Remember the ship will sail after Isha prayer on Tuesday, the first night of Jumad the second."

"You mean Jumad the latter?"

"Hahaha, yes, that one. Head to the ship's chief sailor before you disembark, and present your identification documents to him to place yourself on the passenger list."

"Thank you, but why do you trust me so much?"

"I am a good judge of character and I believe that you are trustworthy. Now, I must find my father before he finds us." With that, she turned and moved toward the captain's chambers, and my eyes followed her until she closed the door behind her.

(8)

Abatshah

Mountains

Yasser Bahjatt ياسر بهجت

Just before dawn of Sunday the fourteenth of Muharram 290 FG

I woke up to the sounds of movement between the branches around us. I opened my eyes to utter darkness. I stretched out my right hand to tap Fida on his shoulder and wake him up. He tapped me back on my shoulder, confirming that he was already awake and heard the same sounds. Fida made some sounds from his throat talking to Heraak. The full moon was no longer in the sky and its light was gone. Deer could sense their surroundings in that darkness. What I feared most was that Jabal's army had found us out that quickly. We had barely made it, after much effort and hardship, to the forest of Al-Othama[1] foothills of the Abatshah Mountains. It was extremely cold and I was furious with Fida for insisting that we not start any fires. Time passed slowly as we waited for Heraak's report regarding the source of movement. As time passed, sounds of movement around us came closer. I pulled my sword and dagger out of their sheaths, and prepared to strike.

"They are animals displaced from the west. Amongst them are a decent number of moose. Heraak will try to find out from them what is going on."

---

[1] Al-Othama—Translation: Great ones.

I returned my weapons to their sheaths. "I will go back to sleep. We need to rest after completing a twenty-day journey in only fifteen days. Wake me if something new happens or if the sun comes out."

Before I finished my sentence, I felt a mouse pass over my body, followed by another, and then a group of rabbits. Then I heard the steps of a much larger animal. I jumped up, and something bumped into me. I think it was a medium-sized moose, which I tried to avoid, causing me to slam into another, much larger, moose, almost pushing my face into the ground, followed by many other bumps and slams. I could barely keep my balance.

"Heraak says we should shield ourselves behind tree trunks, as their numbers are vast and confused. He could not get any useful information out of them regarding what was going on."

I made several screaming sounds addressing Shaheen, and he immediately answered me.

"It is too dark, and Shaheen could not see underneath those trees. He will try to go up and see what is going on at the mountain peak or beyond."

"Tell him to come back by dawn. I do not want anyone to see him, as his movement opposite to those of the animals will raise suspicion."

I screamed a few more screams, and Shaheen replied in agreement.

"I think we arrived on the same night as Jabal's army. These animals must have been displaced

because of the army's campsite on the west side of this mountain." I was yelling so that Fida could hear me over the noise of the animals, but I did not hear any response from him. I resisted my urge to yell even louder, to call him and make sure he was all right, but I kept shut to avoid giving out our location to Jabal's scouts, who, I assume, are in the area now.

Time passed slowly, and animals were still fearfully running around us, away from the Abatshah Mountain. I yelled, "Fida, it is the Jabal."

A few moments later, I felt Fida pushing himself behind the tree trunk I was shielding myself behind.

"And who else, other than Jabal, would do such a thing?"

"No, you do not understand. It is the mountain, Abatshah Mountain. It is the cause of all of this disturbance. These animals surely did not climb the mountain from the west side to flee this way. They all must be from the eastern forests of the mountain, and how can an army terrify all of these animals so that they would flee their homes in this forest?! There are no fires on the peaks of the mountain, otherwise Shaheen would have seen them and told me, nor have we heard any loud noises that might have spooked them this way."

"And how did Abatshah Mountain cause this?"

"It must have been a tremor. That must have been what we felt when we woke up. The mountain shivered."

"The mountain shivered? What nonsense is this?!"

123

"Aren't mountains the totem of Jabal, son of Siraa? He must have communicated with the mountain."

"This is a mountain of solid rock that does not move. How would he make it shiver?!"

"I spent some time with master Hatim, son of Abd Rab Al-Samaa[1], one of the mountaineers' masters. He told us that Uhud Mountain, as well as Al-Noor, had shivered, and that their shivers were outbursts of emotions that came over them."

"And how can Jabal, son of Siraa, do that?!"

"The mountain is not my totem, but the master taught me some methods of connecting emotionally with mountains. Let me try. I might understand what happened to the mountain."

Fida replied, mockingly, "Go ahead. We got nothing better to do for now."

I ignored his mocking tone, and praised Allah and thanked him, then started reciting what Allah would remind me of—verses of mountains—as I tried to open up my senses to feel Abatshah's mountain emotions. With time, feelings of anger—a strange sort of anger such as I had never before felt—mixed with resentment, came over me. In fact, it was more like disrespect.

"I think I know what happened. I think Abatshah Mountain felt Jabal, son of Siraa, because

---

[1] Abd Rab Al-Samaa—Translation: Worshiper of the God of the heavens.

of his strong connection with mountains, as they are
his totem, and the mountain must have felt that the
reason he was here was to start the flames of war, and
his desire to shed the blood of believers. I think the
mountain shivered in anger and dread of such
thoughts."

"I was just about to label you crazy, if it wasn't
for the fact the Heraak just informed me that the
animals were fleeing the foothills because of a tremor,
but how did you communicate with the mountain,
especially since it is not your totem?!"

"I can't communicate with him, but my master
Hatim told me that I possess an ability that is rarely
possessed by someone not from the mountain totem:
the ability to feel mountains' emotions."

"Why did you not inform me of that before?"

"Because I knew you would not believe me, and
would label me as crazy."

I noticed that the situation around us had calmed
down, and that we were no longer besieged by fleeing
animals. Then I heard Shaheen's voice. He informed
me that he had seen the flames of hundreds of
campfires on the foothills of Abatshah Mountain. The
army had indeed set up camp."

"Baz, ask Shaheen to count the army's
campfires."

"He told me they were in the hundreds. I do not
think he can count them with any more accuracy, as
counting was never one of his strong suits. It might
actually be in the thousands, but he would not know

the difference."

"Then we must get to the top of the mountain and find out for ourselves. We must hurry. We will need at least a full day to reach a peak where we can see the west-side foothill and the army's camp."

I looked at the mountain that sparkled under the first threads of dawn. I patted Shaheen on his head when he landed on my left shoulder as I contemplated the hard day ahead of us.

◦✧✧✧✧✧✧✧✧✧◦

Out of exhaustion, I fell on my back after spending the day climbing Abatshah Mountain until we arrived at the nearest point where we could see the vale on its west side. Shaheen stood next to my head as he pecked it to force me to allow him to soar and get closer to the army's camp, while Fida lay next to me, taking a breath and avoiding being seen by anyone. I gestured my agreement to Shaheen after he convinced me that his soaring at that time would not raise any suspicions, as that was the time he used to hunt at. Our mission now was to know the size of the army and its armament. Despite Shaheen's weak mathematical skills, he was very good at estimating distances and areas, so he would size up the area that the army was now occupying and that would give him an idea of the army's approximate size, while Heraak would try to get closer to the army to know its tooling and armament. In the meantime, Fida and

I would observe the soldiers' movements and the camp's division to try and figure out how the army was organized.

We had but a few minutes before sunset. After that, a few hours of moonlight. We had to make use of that time to collect as much information as possible. I rolled over onto my stomach and pulled my saed out of my bag to observe the campsite behind the mountain and document everything I saw. The fires were all over the camp's vast area, soldiers were surrounding them for warmth, and a few scouts— some of whom were equipped with pistols with scopes—monitored the camp's perimeter. One of the guards noticed Shaheen soaring over the camp site. He knelt down on one knee and pointed his pistol at Shaheen. I tried to warn Shaheen, but any sound I made to warn him would reach the soldier and confirm his suspicions that Shaheen was there accompanying a scout, in addition to giving out our location to the entire army. Against my better judgment, I held my breath as I watched the soldier tracking Shaheen through his pistol's scope. Then I saw the flash of his pistol, followed by the exploding sound. I raised my head in panic toward Shaheen, only to find him falling toward the camp. I almost screamed in agony, but Fida's hand on my shoulder brought me back to reality. I shed my tears as I watched my friend fall out of the sky. I pointed my scope toward Shaheen in a desperate attempt to know where he fell, in hopes that I could find a way to save him. My tears froze in my eyes when Shaheen spread his wings before slamming into the ground as he snatched a chicken with his legs from one of the soldiers' hands that he was just about to throw onto the fire to grill, and Shaheen soared high while the soldier kept screaming with anger at him. The soldiers around him exploded with strange, hysterical laughter. I returned my gaze to Shaheen, who flew away from the army toward one of the mountain's peaks that was somewhat far from our location before he disappeared completely into the dark sky.

"I did not know that Shaheen was so witty and a good actor."

"Thank God he survived. I almost lost one of my best friends."

"Thank God. Did you see that pistol that the soldier used before?"

"I heard of a new type of pistols equipped with scopes and the ability to hit targets thousands of feet away. I think they are called snipers."

"We must relay everything we have seen here to my father, write everything so we could send it with Shaheen."

"I wrote all the information we had gathered about the army from divisions, equipment, armament, advanced weaponry, and steam machines carrying the cannons. I screamed with a sharp eagle sound asking Shaheen to come back to our location to get the information regarding the area the camp *occupied to add to my letter that I put into a pod along with a few shadows that we have captured. I tied the pod to one of Shaheen's legs and ordered him to go to Al-Oyoon Al-Hamia and hand it to the Khalifa personally. And just before he took off, I heard several raptors' sounds from different locations around the mountain, and then several flying shadows appeared in the sky of this moonlit night.*

"Go Shaheen as fast as you can. They know we are here. Come on, Baz. We need to run before they get to us."

As we stood up to run, we heard the howling of wolves coming toward us. Losing the wolf totems, the best trackers, will not be easy.

"Heraak says that they are four thousand or so feet away. They must have had a group of scouts up here. We will not be able to see our way in this thick forest that blocks out the moon's light. We will follow Heraak. This will be fun, don't you think?"

"Absolutely. Nothing beats running for your life from a pack of wolves as fast as you can downhill in a thick, dark forest, on the footsteps of a deer."

◦✧✧✧✧✧✧✧✧◦

Our descent that night was one of the hardest things I have done in my life. I had slammed into many tree trunks and fell several times after I tripped over a rock or branch. Fida had better luck than I did because of the skills he had learned from his deer

129

totem regarding the use of all of his senses in darkness to feel the world around him, yet, he also slammed into a few trees and fell a few times. The wolves' sounds were getting closer as time passed. There was a full moon tonight. It was the night of the wolf. No one could out-match the wolves' abilities on such a night. We would not last long this way. They would catch up to us sooner or later.

"Fida, we will not out run them. They are much faster than we are in this darkness. We must find another way."

"Any suggestions?"

"Ask Heraak about their distance."

"A little less than three thousand feet.

"I need him to find us the scent of a beast's dung, such as a bear or a mountain lion."

"What do you plan on doing?"

"We will hide between trees and under branches after we rub ourselves with the dung. The wolves are now tracking us by our scent, and they will surly avoid such beasts' scents."

"Heraak said that we will have to change our direction, and go a few thousand feet into the forest. This will take us away from our escape route."

"Our escape route will not save us. Tell him to lead the way to the dung."

"I do not like the idea of rubbing myself in dung."

"We have no other choice."

Heraak changed our direction from east to

يقطينيا Yaqteenya

northeast. We arrived at a spot that reeked of a very
bad odor, but it wasn't dung; it was a dead body.

"I found it. It is a huge dead bear. What now?"

"Open its guts up and carry it in your bag."

"Are you crazy? Why do we not just hide
underneath it?"

"That will be the first thought of the wolves'
companions: that we came here to hide in this corpse's
odor, which is why we need to rub ourselves with it,
then carry some of it with us as we continue our
escape, then rub ourselves again in a location a few
thousand feet from here and hide."

"My hate for you and your ideas increases with
every word you utter."

I took out my dagger and slashed open the bear's
stomach, letting out odors that I never knew existed. I
took a handful and released it into my bag and so did
Fida, then took a second handful and rubbed my
chest, arms, and legs.

"You need to rub Heraak, too, and don't forget to
carry some extra to rub him with when we hide."

Heraak resisted nervously as he avoided Fida's
fist, but in the end, he submitted and allowed Fida to
rub his body with that filthy substance. He then
started running again, but much slower than
previously, as the scent we covered ourselves in
weakened the Heraak's and Fida's senses of smell,
reducing their ability to move in this darkness. The
pack of wolves was quickly getting closer. They then
stopped for some time. They must have reached the

131

bear's corpse. Then they started to get closer again. When they were about a thousand feet away, I gestured to Fida to spread out and hide away from each other to reduce the chances of being discovered. We took out the scent we carried and rubbed ourselves with it, and then Fida made Heraak lay under a bush and covered him with branches and tree leaves. He then moved to another bush to hide, as did I.

We heard the wolves pass by us, but they slowed down when they came to our location.

"They have lost their scent. They must have changed direction and are moving east again."

"Let us search this location first. They could be hiding somewhere here."

"This is what you said at that rotten corpse. You have wasted our time and caused us to lose their tracks after we were on the verge of catching them. We will not waste any more time. We must find them before they get out of this forest."

"But I am sure…"

"I said we will not waste any time. Head east."

They stormed away from us, and we remained in hiding, in fear that they would turn back. Hardship and fatigue had taken its toll on us, and our bodies tricked us into dozing off without resistance.

(9)
Treachery

ياسر بهجت Yasser Bahjatt

Noon of Thursday the twenty-sixth of Jumad the former 291 FG

I disembarked from Al-Anqaa to find myself in Sibtah's harbor that was stuffed with warships and soldiers. This city was not like Akadeer, as it was a purely military city. Its main purpose, as I understood it from one of the sailors here, was to be an icon of the Ottoman's navy power to terrorize the Europeans, specifically the Spanish. The strange thing was that unlike Akadeer, the walls of this city did not extend into the sea. On the contrary, it was totally exposed, but it was filled with cannons pointing toward the sea. I found out that many skirmishes between the Ottoman and Spanish navies happened in this area, and that the Spanish opened fire on all Ottoman ships that came within range of their cannons, and that was why Al-Anqaa was going to sail on a moonless night, as she would move within range of the Spanish cannons on her way to Osia Harbor.

Jabal Tariq is over there across the sea. I have nine days to visit the mountain, get to Alhambra Palace, about which I have heard so much, and get back here to catch the ship. I changed out of the Ottoman soldier clothes and hid them in an alley. Then I put on my Yaqteenyan clothes. They are much

135

more comfortable and better for fighting if I had to in Spain. I tried hard to find someone who would take me across this sea to Jabal Tariq, but everyone I met would not even entertain the idea, until someone pointed me toward a merchant whom I was told was in the business of smuggling Ottoman products to Spain and vice versa. I found the merchant, who introduced himself as Antonio. I agreed with him that he would get ten dinars to take me to the Spanish side, then back on the night of Tuesday the first of Jumad the latter. He led me to a boat and raised its base to show a hidden compartment that was barely enough for me to hide along with my equipment until we reached the other side. After some time, the boat bumped into something. I think it was another ship. It then stopped completely, and I heard a guy yelling in a strange language. I think it must have been Spanish. Then I heard Antonio reply as he entered into a long discussion before the boat moved again, only to stop again a few short moments later. I waited in my place until Antonio got me out, and then suddenly, without warning, the box lid popped open and I found myself in front of a group of Spanish soldiers pointing their weapons at me. One of them held me by my shirt and raised me up, then threw me outside the boat, as he yelled words I did not understand. I tried to get up, but one of them kicked me in my back, forcing me to the ground face down. Two feet appeared in front of me. I raised my

136

head to see their owner's face. It was Antonio standing next to who, from the looks of things, appeared to be the person in charge of this place.

"What brought you here?" the man asked in perfect Arabic.

"Master Pedro, Duke of Sidonia. He is an Ottoman spy. I saw him disembark from Al-Anqaa in his Ottoman uniform before he came to me in these strange clothes, asking me to transport him here."

"What is his name?"

"I did not ask him, Sir, so that I would not raise his suspicions, but his stuff is on my boat."

Pedro pointed to his soldiers to bring my stuff off the boat, and then spoke fluently in that strange language. Someone tied my hands behind my back, and then raised me harshly to stand on my feet as he pushed me in front of him. I stopped for a moment as I saw that glorious view, as my horizon was filled with Jabal Tariq, as if it was a wall made of pure white pearls. Feelings of grief that filled its stones echoed between my ribs. I could not control myself as my eyes teared up in response to the intensity of those feelings. The soldier hit me on my back to push me forward until we arrived at a building made from the Jabal Tariq's stones, making it seem as part of it. I got to a room near the building where Pedro sat behind a luxurious desk that was in no way comparable to Antarah's desk. This desk was shining, as if polished yesterday. Its smooth wooden surface had no scratches or breaks. Antonio stood next to it.

My stuff was spread all over the floor, and a steel chair sat in the center of the room. The soldier forced me to sit on it, then tied my hands to it. The commander signaled the soldier to leave.

"Why did the Turks send you here?"

"I am not a Turk, and I am not their spy."

"You are a despicable spy, oh ..." he then looked at a paper laying on his desk, and said, as he looked directly into my eyes, and with clear emphasis on every letter, "Abdulqadeer, son of Mohammad Al-Hawazli."

"That is not my name. I am Al-Baz Al-Monqad."

"Liar! Why would you carry this document if that was not your name? What I do not understand is why the Turks sent you. I have captured many of their spies before, but you are the first of such high stature," he said without breaking eye contact.

I did not understand what he meant by "high stature," and I clearly looked puzzled, so he continued. "You think I do not know who you are? You are the son of the scholar Mohammad, son of Ali Akbeel Al- Hawazli, one of the greatest Quran scholars in your country, so for the Turks to send his son to our country, your mission must be much greater than that of a mere spy."

"I told you I am not him. I am..."

I could not complete my sentence, as his fist slammed into my jaw with such force that it almost broke it and forced it out of its place.

138

"As you know, we are a pure people and we do not like lying." He then waved his finger at Antonio as he continued. "That is why we created these pieces of art that force thugs to say the truth."

Antonio opened the doors to the cabinets that lined up the back wall, showing metal tools of all shapes and sizes, the common denominator amongst them all being that they had one or more sharp or pointy edges. A shiver went through my body. Although I understood exactly what those tools were used for, I had never imagined or heard of a human thinking of harming another in such a manner. His eyes turned to savageness as he said, "Do not be in such a hurry. We are not monsters here. We will first beat you with our bare hands," and his fist slammed into the other side of my jaw. I felt dizzy and spat out blood.

"There you are showing your Turkish savagery. How dare you spit on my courtier's floor?" Then he punched me in my lower chest, forcing me to yell in pain.

"Now, let me ask you again. Who are you? And why are you here?"

"I told you, I am Al-Baz Al-Monqad, son of Al-Thib Al-Hakeem, chieftain of the Sherokah clan."

He looked at Antonio. "Did you ever hear of such a name? We always thought that Turks were savages, but now we know they are animals." He followed that with a kick to my chest, forcing me to fall onto my back.

139

I heard steps, then saw Antonio's face clearly panicking as he lifted my chair.

"Let us try this again. Who are you? And why are you here?"

I moaned in pain, and I knew there was no way out of this mess other than playing along with this maniac, and telling him what he wanted to hear, thus lying to him. "You know who I am, and I came to return Al-Andalus to its people."

High-pitched, mocking giggles echoed in the room.

"Return Al-Andalus? To its people? Did you not know that it was its people who handed it over to the Spanish throne? I see you are puzzled. Yes, my father handed over the city of Tarifa to the throne. It is no longer Andalus. It is Spain now. Tell me, how are you to return it? Who is your spy?"

"I do not know. All I can tell you is that I must be in Alhambra Palace in two days with all of my stuff."

"Excellent. You have started to learn honesty. And why are you here?"

"I came to teach the people of this land their religion that you have taken away from them, and help them reclaim it from your throne."

He slapped me as he grinned in anger. "That is how you Turks behave: always pushing your noses where they do not belong. Why concern yourselves with this resistance movement that we have? And what are those tools you carry with you?" he asked,

140

as he pushed my tools that were scattered all over the floor with his feet.

"These are the latest spying and crowd-influencing tools our scientists in Istanbul have conceived, sent with me to teach a group of the resistance how to use them."

Antonio then continued his chat in Spanish and left the room. Antonio came closer to me and released my hands from the chair with clear anxiety, as he avoided looking me in the eyes. It was clear that he felt guilty. I do not think he expected this savagery from Pedro.

"Can I pray Thuhur? I promise to be quick, and not to try to escape."

Antonio looked hesitantly at me. "Very well, but quickly, and I swear if you try to trick me, it will only result in your pain." He pointed at the open cabinets as he said that.

"Can you release my chains?"

"You have to pray with them on, behind your back. I am not a fool."

I stood quickly, faced where I thought southeast would be, and started my prayer. I felt Jabal Tariq's pain, but that pain recessed with every verse I read, and every move I made, and every kneel I made, and when I was done with my prayer, that pain turned into anxious longing.

The moment I was done with my prayer, Antonio pulled me up from my chains to a standing position, as he pushed me outside, where he handed me to a

141

soldier who pulled me away after Antonio spoke to
him. He threw me into a steel cage atop a wagon
pulled by two huge horses. Moments later, Pedro
appeared on a horse. "You will lead us to your
informant so that we can make an example out of
him for those who want to work against the throne."

Then he turned his horse and my wagon followed
him, and with its movement, I felt sadness come over
Jabal Tariq once more, but this time, it was mixed
with anger.

◆⟪⟫⟪⟫⟪⟫⟪⟫◆

What I will say now might seem crazy to you,
but although I was chained in a steel cage, and my
face had a few wounds and bruises, I was happy. Yes,
I was very happy. I am now on my way to Granada.
I am on my way to the starting point, where my
mother's lineage came from, and where the Moors
came to us from, and from there I will bring the
evidence to Yaqteenya to end the strife so that we
would become one family again. Granada was only a
myth, a name to which our history was linked. We
have never seen it, and tomorrow I will be the first
Yaqteenyan to see it. I was preoccupied in my
thoughts and dreams, so I did not notice that the
wagon had stopped. My head slammed into the metal
bars of the cage that I had forgotten I was locked in. I
looked around to scan the area. We were on a paved
path inside a thick forest, and darkness was moving

in. *It seems I had not paid attention for some time now and did not feel anything happening around me. It seemed that a number of soldiers had joined us, making us more like a convoy. They were now moving in every direction. I think they were making sure they could camp there for the night. Moments later, they came back, signaling with their hands what appeared to mean that it was safe; the rest of the soldiers prepared the camp and started fires. And with the first fire started, I was surprised to find Pedro standing directly in front of me.*

"We will stay here for the night. I ordered my soldiers to release their arrows directly at your heart if you tried to escape, so please do not try that. Your departure will cause me so much pain." He could not contain himself as he burst into hysterical laughter, then sat near one of the campfires.

Yasser Bahjatt ياسر بهجت

(10)
Mantiq Al-Tayr

ياسر بهجت Yasser Bahjatt

يقطينيا Yaqteenya

Thursday the first of Safar 289 FG

I was roaming around on the trees in the corner of Qurtuba's main square, my mind occupied with what awaited me while Awqab and Shaheen, my two raptor brothers, watched me from above on its branches. They were a very strange sight for anyone observing us. Awqab was the greatest eagle I had ever seen. He was almost the size of a big sheep. When extended, his wingspan was more than four arms, while Shaheen did not grow beyond the size he was the day he fell out of his nest. He was hardly the size of a small kitten; his extended wings were no more than four spans. The square was getting crowded. I did not expect this at all. I was expecting it to be a simple event, like all other performances done by any examinee, but it seems that I stepped into hot water when I agreed to Fida's proposal that we both present our performances together. Everyone must be here to watch the Khalifa's son. I awakened from my thoughts when I unconsciously turned and held a fist that was speeding toward me.

"Why all of this tension, Baz? You have just been able to predict my fist attack, even though you were not paying any attention. If your performance today is half as good, you will no doubt pass," said Fida cheerfully.

"I did not predict your fist attack. I was warned by Shaheen, and I am not worried about the performance, but as you know, I am not one who enjoys showing off like you."

Fida opened his mouth to respond with one of the proverbs that he received every day from his tutors, but the call to start that had echoed throughout the square delayed him for a moment before he said, "Do not pay much attention to the crowds. We have practiced this many times in the past few weeks." He then looked upward as he said, "Tell him that there is nothing to be worried about.

"You know they will not understand a word you say."

He shook his head carelessly as he moved toward the square's center, followed by Heraak and Hakoom, I followed them and Shaheen came down to stand on my shoulder, while Awqab soared high as he hovered around the square as he kept an eye on me.

Fida stood facing the stage, Heraak and Hakoom right behind him, and me on his right. A group of top Yaqteenyan masters sat on stage, including my master, Saqr Al-Akaber and next to him, my teacher, Qutabah Al-Andalusi; one of the most famous warriors of Yaqteenya, then the army's general, Al-Muthana; then Fida's master, whose name I forget, but he was by far the best deer totem master. He had gone to Qurtuba from his town far northwest of Yaqteenya when he knew of the Khalifa's son's totem, *so that he could personally teach him; then master Shamikh, son of Wedyan Al-Kamohi[1], the master of the mountain totem in Qurtuba, along with three other masters whom I did not know, but I assumed they were other masters from the same totems to give their opinions to our masters regarding what we would present to them.*

The crowds clapped when master Saqr stepped forward.

"My Yaqteenyan brothers and sisters, dear masters, al-salmu alikum wa rahmato Allah wa barakatuh. I have been honored for the past few months to have a trainee who is one of the brightest children of the raptor totem, and my brother master of the deer totem was also honored with such a trainee, not only because of his blood line, but also his unrivaled skill, and it is my great honor to welcome you all to watch what they have prepared for us. We are here today because of their request to receive the following Ijazas: Ijazah of raptors, Ijazah of combat and knighthood, and Ijazah of mountains for Al-Baz Al-Monqad; and Ijazah of deer, and Ijazah of combat and knighthood for Fida Al-Deen."

The master stopped talking for a while as he looked over the crowds before he continued. "I presume, based on the number of audience members here today, that most of you know how rare it is for two people to request presenting in a single

---

[1] Shamikh, son of Wedyan Al-Kamohi—Translation: Standing tall son of Valleys of the Kamohi clan.

performance for their Ijazah, especially if they were from two different totems, but it is also the first Ijazah request where a person combines more than one Ijazah in the same performance. Never in our history has anyone been able to get an Ijazah in more than one totem, and the puzzlement does not stop there. As you know, totem Ijazas' performances usually happen in nature or in open areas. This will be the first performance I hear of that happened within the city. For all of that. I request that Fida and Al-Baz start their performance, as I can barely hide my excitement."

A cloud of silence engulfed the square, and time passed slower than usual, before Fida poked me with his elbow.

"Our honorable masters…" then I looked around me… "Brothers and sisters, today, in hopes that our masters would honor us by granting us the Ijazas we have requested, we will present to you a performance that will show our mastery of the skills required for those Ijazas. But today we will not show off our skills of working with our totems in the traditional way, where the totem in my case, for example, would be used for scouting and surveillance. Rather, we will show how we can take that relationship to a much more complicated level." Then I turned toward Al-Muthana and asked, "May I battle your best soldier?"

He nodded before he pointed to one of his soldiers

who worked in the Khalifa guard. He stepped forward and stood in front of me in his full armament.

"May I request that we start without weapons? You may utilize your totem, if you wish."

The soldier took off his sword and dagger. "And what use would my totem be in a fight?"

"That choice is up to you. I hope you fight with all the skill and strength that you have."

The soldier stood in a battle-ready posture and locked his eyes onto mine before he stormed toward me in fast steps. He balled up his fist tightly. I did not move from my place until he was about a step away from me and his fist was blazing toward me when he was surprised by Awqab dropping from the sky directly in front of his face with his wings spread wide. He lost his balance when his fist did not hit its mark after I had moved over to hit his back with my fist, forcing him to the ground.

"As you can see, I used my totem to surprise my opponent and distort his view at the same time. That caused the opponent to continue his attack and lose focus when he did not strike his expected target."

The crowds clapped. I helped the soldier stand to his feet, then I gestured to him to attack again, but he nodded in refusal, and he signaled me to start the attack. I moved toward him in slow, confident steps while our eyes locked. My steps grew faster as I got closer to him. When I was a couple of steps away, I raised my left fist, then Awqab broke our eye contact

151

as I stepped to my right while the soldier was confused. By the time he could see in front of him again for a brief moment, he discovered that I was no longer in front of him. Then his eyesight was interrupted again by Shaheen's wings, and he felt my right fist against his left side.

"Locking eyes with your opponent causes him confusion when that connection is interrupted for any reason. This gives you the ability to easily surprise your opponent."

The soldier snarled as he dug his feet into the ground. "Can't you fight me while I see you? Do you need to hide behind your totems' wings?"

I turned to face him. He was five or more feet away. "How about we use some weapons?" Fida tossed us two wooden swords. The soldier smiled with half a face after he picked up the sword in his right hand. Shaheen landed on my left arm, while Awqab landed on my cape right behind my head. The soldier stormed toward me with utter speed and fury to swing his sword toward my head with extreme violence. I quickly stepped back to avoid his strike, and with my step, Awqab flapped his powerful wings to pull me hard to the back. At that very moment, I released my left fist toward his right arm, which was holding the sword, and with it, Shaheen was frantically flapping his wings to add his power and speed to my arm. My fist struck the soldier's arm; he screamed in pain and his grip on his sword loosened.

Shaheen did not stop. He let go of my arm to continue flying toward the soldier's fist to peck it violently with his beak, forcing him to let go of the sword. Shaheen completed his flight with a quick maneuver around the soldier's arm to hit the sword's grip toward me. I caught the sword as I continued a full circle around my left foot, and struck the soldier's back with my sword and stabbed him with his sword while my back was facing him. The square rumbled with clapping and yelling.

"The addition of my totem's strength and movement to my strength gives me the ability to perform movements that would be impossible to perform on my own. Additionally, their movement with me adds fighting advantages that my opponent does not expect, especially that he never knew were possible, thus adding to the element of surprise. Also, sensing the gravel underneath us allows me to know my opponent's real stance and the direction of his next move."

I flipped the two swords in my hand and raised their grips toward the soldier. "Thank you, Brother, for this duel." He took them from my hand before he stood in respect and left the arena.

"That is enough from you, Baz. Fida, please step forward and show us what you have."

Fida stood facing the stage and nodded in respect. Behind him stood Heraak, calm and respectful. He was no longer that baby moose that we found in the woods. His shoulder was almost as high as Fida's head and his horns had grown out more than an arm's length on each side of his head. Next to him, Hakoom stood nervously as he hit the ground with his feet, and swung his head as he made annoying rumbling sounds. A deer his size, almost as big as Heraak, especially when his horns were much bigger and branched out with sharp pointy ends, was not a creature you wanted to face, especially when it was that nervous.

"My honored masters, my presentation will not depend on surprise and agility that my brother, Al-Baz, depended upon, but on strength and confrontation." He then looked into Qutabah's eyes and continued. "For that, Sir, I would request that you send out three of your best fighters to face me and my two brothers, and I would hope that they are not from the Khalifa's guard, so that they would not have any reservations about assaulting the Khalifa's son."

Al-Muthana smiled and Qutabah signaled three of his students. They moved into the arena, and surrounded Fida and his two brothers.

"Would you like to fight with or without weapons?"

"Your two brothers are armed. There is no escape from all of us using weapons to make it a fair fight."

Fida pointed at me and I handed a wooden sword to each of them. One of them insisted on having two swords, so I returned to Fida with one more sword, *and with Heraak and Hakoom's helmets.*

"These two helmets are to protect my brothers' horns from breaking at the skull," said Fida, explaining to his opponents.

"And to ensure that we do not have any fatalities, I have commanded my two brothers to not use their horns for any strikes, therefore, I would appreciate it if any of you touched by any of their horns would withdraw from the fight because in a real fight, it would strike him dead."

The fighters attacked Fida and his brothers. Hakoom snared and ran toward one of them, leaning his head down to ram him, and when he got close, he raised his head as he violently twisted his nick to pick up his opponent's sword with his horn and tossed it far into the crowds while maintaining his assault, slamming his body into the man and throwing him a few feet back. In the meantime, Heraak had also disarmed his opponent, but his opponent was fast and avoided his body. Fida had engaged the third fighter in a fast and powerful sword fight that, at first, seemed uneven, as Fida only had one sword, while his opponent was attacking him with two, but Fida was blocking the attacks from both swords with agility and skill on his sword's edge, following it sometimes with kicks or punches.

"Leave the deer. Let us all attack Fida," he said as he attacked Fida with both his swords at once. Heraak pushed his right horn to block both swords, while Hakoom blocked the path of one of the other

155

fighters with his body. Fida leaned on his Hakoom's back as he pushed himself over it to attack the fighter from the sky, throwing him to the ground, then stabbing his chest with his wooden sword. Fida stood and circled around Hakoom to face the double swords man who jogged toward him. Fida pointed with one of the fingers on his left hand. Hakoom leaned on his two arms as he struck with his legs. And one of them hit the fighter, throwing him far away. The last fighter slid on the ground under Heraak and Hakoom to stand right behind Fida and wrap his arms around Fida's neck and waist. Fida tried to escape his grip, but to no avail, so he leaned forward to flip onto his back, falling to the ground on top of his attacker, forcing him to let him go from the pain of the collision. As soon as Fida moved from on top of him, Heraak's feet fell on both sides of the fighter.

"If we were in a real fight, those hooves would have been in your guts or chest."

The square rumbled with yells, whistles, and applause from the audience, until Qutabah asked them to calm down.

"What an amazing presentation and performance, but tell me, how were you able to train your brothers on this fighting performance and coordinate their performance with your fighting?"

"What we learn from our totem masters is how to communicate with our brothers from our totem through specific sounds that are all derived out of the book (Mantiq Al-Tayr[1]) written by Master Kinan, son of Abd Rab Ah-Jibaal Al-Ajeeby, allowing us to build simple pronounceable sentences, but my brother, Al-Baz, wanted to interact with his brothers in a way that allowed him to transfer much more complicated ideas and to do so much quicker."

"After reading and studying everything written about communicating with totems, I found that the bases for all of them was that communicating with them was vocal or, in the case of mountains and trees, the belief that what we were sensing from them represented words, as we humans were used to assuming that the pronounced word was what (Mantiq Al-Tayr) meant, but I thought that, more accurately, here was the mental logic[2], as birds and other creatures see the universe around them through a view and logic that is surely different from ours. Therefore, if we tried to think through their logic, we would be able to communicate with them in a much more accurate and complex manner. That allowed me to take everything I learned from my master and build upon it to make it more detailed and faster, to the point that it is almost psychic, like what happens to me and Fida when we fight side by side, and that

---

[1] Mantiq Al-Tayr—Translation: Mantiq can mean pronunciation, Al-Tayr means birds, loosely translated to "Birds' speech."

[2] In Arabic, the word Mantiq also means logic. What Al-Baz is referring to here is that (Mantiq Al-Tayr) was used in the holy Quran, and was referenced in most Yaqteenyan studies related to totems as the bases for communicating with them. By changing the inferred meaning, he opened up a new way to understand his relationship with his totem.

was why we wanted to use them in fighting and movement synchronization between us and our brothers, as such application would be the best proof of such an idea."

The deer totem master stepped forward. "I never thought that someday someone would reach such a level of communication with our brothers, and it is my honor that the first to be able to do so would be linked to my lineage. We have agreed to grant Fida Al-Deen, son of Wadda Al-Moori, an Ijazah for the deer totem, as well as an Ijazah for combat and knighthood. We have also agreed to grant Al-Baz Al-Monqad, son of Al-Thib Al-Hakeem, an Ijazah for the raptor totem, as well as an Ijazah for combat and knighthood. As for Al-Baz's Ijazah for the mountain totem, although Master Shamikh was impressed with Al-Baz's performance and his puzzlement over him sensing the square's gravel, he regrets that he must reject his request for an Ijazah."

My master gave me the ring of the raptor totem, a shiny silver feather wrapped around my finger, while Fida received a deer totem's ring, two wide wooden horns.

Crowds flocked toward us to congratulate us on our success and discuss what we had done in our performance. After a little while, the crowds around us disappeared. Fida looked at me and asked, "Why don't you seem happy with what you have achieved today? No one has ever received two Ijazas from the *same performance before. Is that not cause enough to celebrate?"*

"I guess so, but why did master Shamikh refuse to grant me the Ijazah? What more proof does he need to that I possessed the abilities of the mountain totem than me sensing tens of stones all at once and with fighting speed?" Then my thoughts drifted as I carried my heavy steps back home.

Yasser Bahjatt ياسر بهجت

(11)
Nerja

ياسر بهجت Yasser Bahjatt

The night of Saturday the twenty-seventh of Jumad the former 291 FG

The sky was pouring when we arrived at a small coastal city. We headed toward the military center of the city to spend the night. Pedro passed by my cage on his way to his quarters, and said, mockingly, "I hope you enjoy our hospitality for the night."

He moved on and disappeared from my sight. One of the soldiers opened the iron door of the cage that I had spent the last two days in. He viciously pulled me from the chain that handcuffed me. I fell face first into the mud. I was surprised to see a soldier's face fall in front of me covered in fear and pain. I quickly stood up, to find out that seven soldiers had fallen to the ground, and five others had arrows sticking out of different parts of their bodies. The other ten were shielding themselves behind their horses or the cage where I was detained. Suddenly five warriors came out of the folds of darkness to attack the soldiers by striking their necks and chests. The Spanish soldiers froze in surprise and four more fell dead; three others were wounded, one severely. I jumped one of the soldiers with an attack to the back of his head with both of my fists and the chains between them rumbled with a frightening sound when it slammed into his head. I pulled one of the soldier's swords to join the

163

fight. Using the sword was extremely difficult; I had to hold it with both hands, which were chained together. All of this, in addition to the weight of the metal chains, negatively affected my sword's movement speed, but at least I was able to block strikes and keep some of the soldiers from their assailants, making the fight more even. I was so busy fighting and trying to stay alive that I do not recall the details of the fight itself. All I remember is that the fight stopped as abruptly as it started, and all the Spanish soldiers were killed, while one of their assailants was badly wounded.

"Are you all right?"

I was astonished when I heard that simple phrase spoken in broken Arabic. My astonishment was not only due to the use of Arabic here in Spain, but also because of the feminine voice that said it. One of the assailants was a woman, and I did not notice that until that moment. She repeated her question once more, but this time her tone of voice carried some obvious concern.

"Are you all right? Were you inured? Do you need medical attention?"

I smiled at her questions and raised my hands in front of my face. "I do not need medical attention, but I need these shackles removed."

"We will remove your hands from the shackles, but right now, we must run."

"Agreed, but I need my stuff and weapons," I said

164

as I pointed toward the cart that was carrying my things.

She signaled one of her assistants. He accompanied me to the cart, where we found a few extra boxes along with the bundle that holds my stuff. Her assistant spoke to her in Spanish; she smiled and signaled the other two men to carry the wounded to the cart.

"We take all of the carts, duke money, and things."

She hopped onto the front of the cart. I followed her while the rest of the men hopped in the back. She whipped the horses to storm away.

◦❖❖❖❖❖❖❖◦

It seems that Al-Baz had intentionally written the dialogue of these Spanish as they had pronounced it in their broken Arabic. I, however, will pass it on to you in proper language to ensure that you do not misunderstand the events.

◦❖❖❖❖❖❖❖◦

She raised the blindfold that she had wrapped around my eyes in fear of my knowing the road to where she was taking me. I found myself at a cave's narrow entrance that was barely noticeable for those who do not know of it. The men carried their wounded comrade into the cave, while others came out and spoke to the woman before they carried the boxes and my bundle inside, as well. The woman whipped the horses to escape into the forest.

"We shall stay here for the night. Only a few know the location of this cave and most of them are affiliated with our group."

"Thank you for saving me. May I have the honor of knowing your name?"

"I am Sara, and we are the children of the resistance. We were told by our informant that they had captured an Ottoman spy of high stature, so we came to save you."

"I am not an Ottoman spy. I am Yaqteenyan."

"Yaqteenyan? Never heard of such a country. Are you allies of the Ottomans? I do not understand. Our informant told us that you were Abdulqadeer, son of Mohammad Al-Hawazli."

"I am not Abdulqadeer. Would you allow us to get out of this rain and into your cave, where I can explain this situation?"

"Sure, come on in," she said, as she theatrically gestured toward the cave.

I had to bend my back to enter from that narrow opening. I stood in awe of the amazing beauty of what I saw: Stone columns dangled from the ceiling as if melted wax, and the flickering fire flames only added to its beauty and awe.

"That was my exact feeling when I saw it for the first time. How amazing is the creation of the lord."

166

"I have never seen or heard of anything like this before."

"This is our hideout, where we gather. I will take you on a tour after you meet our leader and tell him of your mission. He impatiently awaits you."

She led me through the caverns, and I looked around in awe of the cave's beauty and structure, until I stopped in front of a wall with extreme astonishment.

"These look like the drawings in Yaqteenya's caves, drawn by my ancestors thousands of years ago. How could such resemblance be possible?!"

"These caves are filled with myriads of drawings of different shapes and skill levels. We are near David's chambers. Come on. He awaits you."

We arrived to a tight cavern on the far edge of the cave. On one side was a mattress where an old man laid. Sara made a sound to let the man know of our arrival before she greeted him and helped him to sit up as she whispered in his ear.

"You are Abdulqadeer, son of Mohammad Al-Hawazli?"

"No, Sheikh.[1] I am not him. I am Al-Baz Al-Monqad, son of Al-Thib Al-Hakeem, chieftain of the Sherokah clan, one of many Yaqteenyan clans."

"I am an old man, and am very knowledgeable of areas and clans of the Ottoman nation, yet I have never heard of Yaqteenya or the Sherokah clan

---

[1] Sheikh: Sometimes refers to an old man, others to a master or scholar, and sometimes to a clan's chieftain.

167

before."

"We are neither of the Ottoman nation, nor associated with them in any way."

"Why, then, do you carry their documents? And why has Duke Pedro detained you?"

"That is a long story."

"We have the time. Neither of us is going anywhere in this heavy rain."

"All I can tell you is that I am on a mission to document what is happening in Al-Andalus and the Ottoman nation, and that my mission is of the utmost importance. It could mean the life or death for thousands of my people."

"What do you mean by 'document'? Do you write down everything we say and do? And to whom do you pass it?"

"Would you mind if I show you? That would be much easier than telling you."

He nodded in agreement. I looked at Sara and asked, "Would you mind if I got my things?"

"She will go, while you stay here," and he signaled to her, and she left the room.

"Tell me, Baz, where is Yaqteenya?"

"Excuse me, Sheikh. Its secret has been hidden from you for about three centuries, and I cannot let anyone know of its location."

"You mean to say that it has been hidden from us since the fall of Grenada? I heard my father tell of a legend of a few Andalucians who had escaped to a

land filled with goods beyond the sea of darkness, and that they were going to return someday to save us from this ordeal. Was he talking about Yaqteenya? I thought it was but a story we told our kids when they sleep to plant hope into their hearts."

"Do you mind if we continue this discussion when Sara returns with my tools so that I can document everything that is said here?"

"Here, take this pen, ink, and paper, if you want to put it all down." He raised a bunch of papers scattered around him and pointed to an inkwell in the corner.

"That is not what I meant. I told you that everything would be clarified when you see my tools and how they work."

"Very well, son. I will wait. You have intrigued me to see those tools of yours."

Minutes passed slowly, while David and I looked at each other without speaking, awaiting Sara's return. I took the bundle from her the moment she got back and stirred its contents to look for hakee. I pulled out the hakee, along with a few wooden rods and a spool of silk thread. I plugged one of the rods into the hakee, and connected one of its ends to the thread, and hung the spool on its holder in the hakee. I rotated the hakee's handle a few times, enough for knitting an hour or so of speech. I then sat the hakee in front of the old man, David.

"The hakee will knit our voices onto this rod so that we can listen to it any time after that."

169

"Are you mocking me?! How would a silk thread along with a wooden rod preserve our voices?!"

"Try. I will command it to start knitting. Then we start talking. After that, I will make it repeat everything we said to you." I then pressed the knitting button for the rod to rotate and knit the thread around it.

"Tell me, Sheikh David, who are you? And what are you doing here?"

"We are the Islamic resistance in Spain, the descendants of the Andalucians who ruled this land under the flag of unity more than three centuries ago?"

"What of your ancestors' stories of that era do you remember?"

"As I told you earlier, there is this legendary story. It's told slightly different than the one told by the Spanish. It goes like this: Al-Zaghabi never overthrew his father from power, rather his father had put him in charge as he went to find safe land, and had returned a year later, only to find his son had been captured. He then ruled Granada for three years, where he worked with other Andalucian kingdoms to transport people from Al-Andalus to a new land that he had discovered. He moved to that land and left his brother in charge for two years. His brother sent a secret letter to his nephew, agreeing to the Spanish terms, and returned to rule Granada. After that, Al-Zaghabi spent five years trying to

170

preserve Granada, up to the day it fell. He wept for its loss, and pretended, in front of the Spanish, that he had left for Morocco. He then secretly vanished to go to the land which his father had found."

I pressed the stop button, then took a bottle out of my bundle that contained liquid gum of a honey color. I cut the thread and fixed its end to the rod, then removed the rod from the hakee to dip it in the gum, and raised it to drip the excess gum into the bottle. I shook the rod until the gum completely solidified. I returned the rod to its place in the hakee, and pulled out a tube from my bundle that I fixed into a hole on the hakee's side. I brought the tube close to Sheikh David. "Put this tube in your ear."

The old man took the hakee, and placed the tube's end into his ear. I pressed the echo button and the rod started turning, and David's face turned to fear. He almost threw the hakee away before he pulled the tube out of his ear and push the hakee toward Sara, who took it and did the same, and her astonishment was no less apparent on her facial gestures than his was.

"What magic is this?! How would a machine of metal and a rod of wood knitted with a silk thread recall our voices and echo them?!"

"That is hard to explain, but I assure you, it is not magic or Jinn. It is science, based on the natural order Allah placed in his universe."

I then took out the saed from my bundle, and pointed it toward the old man and pressed the spray. I pulled out the cloth that was inside of it and handed it over to the old man. A tear slipped his eye when it fell on the cloth.

"How? This is not a mirror. How would a cloth reflect my image?"

"It is not reflecting an image. It had captured your shadows. If Sara looked at it now, she would see your shadows, not her image."

Sara grabbed the cloth from David's hand. She placed her hand on her mouth in astonishment the moment she saw what was on it. She kept switching her gaze between David and the cloth.

"This is impossible! How did you do that?!"

"Science has advanced a lot in Yaqteenya. I can teach you how to make these tools, under the condition that you help me reach Alhambra Palace."

"And what use would we have for such tools? How would it help us resist the Spanish?"

"First, it will help you document everything you know of Al-Andalus and the stories of your ancestors before they are forgotten, so that your children will hear them and be able to pass them on, in addition to preserving the faces of those participating in this resistance so that they would be remembered."

"And second?"

"Second, these tools will allow your scouts to capture the shadows of the locations you are monitoring. This will help your leadership better understand the situation much more than written or verbal accounts. As one of our wise men said, a shadow averts a thousand verses. As for the hakee, if you can hide it in the chambers of one of their leaders, it might be able to knit what is said there for you to hear later."

David and Sara exchanged glances, and then she said, "Very well. We will help you."

"I have four nights and as many days to return to Al-Anqaa in Sibtah."

"We need a day to reach Granada, and three days to return to Jabal Tariq. When exactly will you teach us how to make and use those tools?"

"We start immediately, and I will teach you on our way and every night."

"But that is not enough time. You must stay a few extra days."

"I do not have the time. I must return before Al-Anqaa sails. Will you help me or should I go alone?"

She hesitated for a moment, exhaled with frustration, and then said, "We accept. We have no choice. What skills do you need so that I can gather those who can learn from you?"

"An alchemist, a scope maker, and a clock maker."

"We have two of them in the cave—an alchemist and a scope maker—but as for the clock maker, we can meet him in Granada. I will also join you."

"One last request before we start?"

She exhaled with clear annoyance. "What else?"

"Honestly, I have two requests. First, I need to answer nature's call. Where can I do that in this

173

cave? And second, I am hungry. Can I have some food?"

She smiled shyly, embarrassed and a little ashamed of her rudeness, and then answered, "Hahaha, sure. Follow me and we shall arrange everything for you."

(12)
The Regiment

ياسر بهجت Yasser Bahjatt

Wednesday the twenty-fourth of Muharram 290 FG

This morning, we arrived at Al-Oyoon Al-Hamia village, where we met the Khalifa's army that had arrived there the day before. Warriors from more than twenty-three clans from around Yaqteenya gathered there to join the ranks of the Khalifa, and by doing so, announcing their allegiance to the Khalifa and refusal of Jabal's demands. I quickened my steps toward the Khalifa's tent to make sure that Shaheen had arrived safely and I was followed by Fida. When we arrived at the tent, one of the two soldiers guarding it signaled us and said, "The Khalifa had sent for you. He is waiting inside."

Fida fixed his suit as he entered and I was right behind him. Everyone suddenly stopped talking.

"Thank God for your safe return. You have done well. The information you gathered was extremely important," said the Khalifa. His statement that Shaheen had arrived with the information comforted me.

In the tent were the chieftains, including my father, as well as the army's general and a few of the army's captains. The Khalifa asked the general to start. "The information we received shows that six to nine tribes have joined Jabal's army, five of which we are certain of: Nafojah, Abatshah, Comanish, Aajeeb,

177

and Shiyoon. Based on the estimations we received from Fida, his army has about half the men of ours or slightly more, but his armament is more advanced than ours, especially his marksmen and their ability to affect the battle's outcome from afar."

"It is clear that he has been preparing for this battle for some time now. This confirms our suspicions that his desire for power was not a sudden act. How dare he impose himself to rule us when it is clear that the Yaqteenyan clans have chosen the rule of the Moors? We shall decimate him and his army, as they are no match for our numbers," said the chieftain of the Mohakah clan, clearly angry and full of wrath.

"We have argued about this many times, son of Talh, and we have all agreed that I will preach to Jabal's army before the fighting starts that Allah may bring them or some of them back to their senses and we avert the shed of blood. Now, however, we are here to discuss the division of the army and the tasks of each clan in this battle, if Allah set for it to happen," my father replied decisively, then nodded to the army's general to go on.

"We do not yet know where we will face Jabal's army, but I have no doubt that he will utilize his superior marksmanship to win the battle. That means that his marksmen brigade will be standing behind the lines of engagement and most probably atop of a hill or nearby mountain. We will not be able to reach them through traditional means. That is why we will

assemble a regiment of ten men to sneak in at night to the marksmen's location before the battle starts. As for the ground faceoff, we shall utilize our superior numbers to attack him on multiple fronts, so that he would lose focus."

"Excuse me, but did you say that Jabal's marksmen brigade will face a regiment of ten soldiers? Who are those ten? And how are they to face an entire brigade?" Fida asked.

"That is correct. I did say ten soldiers. As for who they are, well, that is the regiment's captain's task."

"And who is the regiment's captain?"

"Al-Baz Al-Monqad Al-Sheroki."

All eyes turned to me, as I blinked stupidly. "Me?!"

"Yes. You are the only one capable of assembling this regiment and preparing it for this mission."

"And how am I to do that?"

"Your fighting abilities, especially your use of your totem. You must find nine other soldiers from this army to add to your regiment and train them to use their totems, as you do."

"That is impossible. I cannot train anyone to do that in two weeks. I need at least six months just to get them to the level where they can perfectly communicate with their totem. Then we need to develop their joint skills, helping them find their own style of combined fighting, which totally depends on the skills and abilities of both the soldier and his totem."

179

"Did you not teach that in Qurtuba? Search the
army for soldiers who had attended your classes, and
choose from amongst them."

"But that class only lasted for five months,
and…"

"We shall find you your regiment and will not let
you down." Fida interrupted me, throwing me a
flaming gaze to bite my tongue. The army's general
went on allocating the tasks for the upcoming battle
between the army's divisions and clans.

◈◇◈◇◈◇◈◇◈◇◈

Fida was really excited for this regiment. It was
our chance to show the effectiveness of our new
method of communicating with animals, and also to
prove that we were capable of carrying the
responsibility of difficult missions. We spent the next
two weeks searching for my regiment's soldiers and
training them, until, other than myself, Fida, and
our totems, we reached eight men and their totems. I
did not know any of their clans because the Khalifa
commanded that we leave our clans aside. We are all
Yaqteenyans, Saab son of Qada[1] with his bear totem
Fazza[2], they were a strange sight for the beholder.
Saab was short, wide shouldered, well built, carrying
a strange lance with four spikes added to its tip. I

---

[1] Saab, son of Qada—Translation: Difficult son of (fate or judgment).
[2] Fazza—Translation: Terrifier.

180

could not tell how old he was. The soldiers whispered of his skill with his strange weapon; that he had beaten five soldiers in a few moments, and Fazza was a huge bear, with dark brown fur. Saab's head could barely be seen behind Fazza's back when he was standing on all fours. Imagine how they would look if Fazza stood on his legs. Amer, son of Khaldoon, was a tall skinny young man. I could tell from his slang that he was from Joddah village on the banks of the Sultan's lake in the western desert. I had never before seen anyone move with such agility and smoothness. I suspected that he was a descendant of one of the legendary soldiers of the battle of the palms, his totem was a giant spider named Shawk.[1] I had never seen his kind before; when standing on all eight legs, he occupied an area equal to an open palm, and when he gets angry, he would stand on four legs while raising the others to the sky. He said that he had found him on one of his trips to the land of Kinanah,[2] above Yaqteenya after he had passed its pyramids and great river amongst the banana trees. He said that his poison would paralyze a man in a few seconds. Additionally, his body was crawling with spiders of all sizes and colors. Our fifth was Salb, son of Al-Hakam[3], a big guy, but he was an unbeaten wrestler. I think only Fazza was capable of wrestling him. He claims, despite his big body, that he could race his

---

[1] Shawk—Translation: Thorns.
[2] Kinanah in Arabic is one of the names of the land of Egypt.
[3] Salb, son of Al-Hakam—Translation: Solid son of the judge.

181

totem alligator Sarab,[1] whose first impression was
that he was smaller than his kin, but he had a
strange ability to move and disappear in water,
especially if it was shallow, to truly be a mirage. The
sixth was Fahad son of Al-Awam,[2] He was our eldest
of more than six hundred moons. Gray hair consumed
most of his head and bushy beard. His astonishing
speed when climbing, despite his age, tells me that he
is from one of the mountainous clans. His totem was
a mountain lion named Buraaq,[3] extremely fast and
agile, and has been with him for more than seven
years. Shihaab, son of Bareeq Al-Nojoom,[4] was the
other raptor, a dignified young man who was a
master of using daggers and throwing knifes. His
totem was an extremely black owl called Layl.[5] There
is no way you can spot him at night, especially if he
shut his eyes. Tiryaq, son of Abq Al-Masaa,[6] was our
healer, a master of swords. He inherited healing from
his ancestors long before the Moors got to Yaqteenya.
His totem was a scorpion named Hood,[7] who was
always on his sword, if the sword did not strike his

---

[1] Sarab—Translation: Mirage.

[2] Fahad, son of Al-Awam—Translation: Leopard son of the
swimmer.

[3] Buraaq was the name of the creature the prophet Mohammad—
peace be upon him—rode on his trip to Jerusalem.

[4] Shihaab, son of Bareeq Al-Nojoom—Translation: Shooting star son
of Stars' twinkle.

[5] Layl—Translation: Night.

[6] Tiryaq, son of Abq Al-Masaa—Translation: Antidote son of
fragrance of evening.

[7] Hood: Is the name of a prophet of ancient Arabia, who is mentioned
in the Qur'an.

opponent, Hood's tail surely would. Badr, son of Haleem,[1] was a quiet man, to the point that you would not notice he was around. He was not social, as he did not like to talk or mingle with others. He was an excellent marksman, with both a bow and a pistol. That is why the general provided him with one of the few snipers they were able to get their hands on. His totem was Naab.[2] It was his exact opposite. He moved all the time and could not stop barking to the point of annoyance, and finally Qabid,[3] terrifyingly-experienced killer. I am sure he could hardly wait for this battle to start to release his dormant daemon. I could almost see his blood thirst in the glare of his eyes. The soldier's whisper of stories from his life would make the hair stand up on the back of your neck. His totem was named Hasss. I've never seen it unwrapped around his left arm.

◆◇◆◇◆◇◆◇◆

Al-Baz's description of his regiment's soldiers intrigued me. I remember having previously read their descriptions. This pushed me to search the other Yaqteenyan scrolls that I had found, and, as I suspected, I found other documents about them or others' notes about them. I will mention them in my upcoming messages.

---

[1] Badr, son of Haleem—Translation: Full moon son of Patient.
[2] Naab—Translation: Fang.
[3] Qabid—Translation: Hold firmly in his fist.

183

◆☆☆☆☆☆☆☆☆◆

"What you learned in my class was to help you understand the logic of your totems and, therefore, enhance your ability to communicate with them, but that alone will not allow you to use them in battle. Most animals, by nature, do not like to interact with humans or face them, except in the extreme situation when the animal feels his, his children's, or his food's safety is threatened. That is why they will usually ignore your requests to do so. During the next few days, we will work on building the trust relationship between you and your totems by diving into their logic to the point where you can get them to get over that barrier when you ask them to; the next level would be for your totem to react to you as if they were an extension of you."

"But wouldn't that be breaking the trust we built?" asked Badr.

"It is so, if you lied to them regarding your objective of such request or how dangerous it is."

"But in a fight, you need speed of movement. How are we to explain the objective and risks of each move to our totems during a fight?" asked Qabid, puzzled.

"That is part of the trust you shall build with your totem. In my case, with Shaheen and Awqab, for example, we had agreed that I would give them all the details when I had the time to do so, but I reduce *only the risk and importance levels when I do not have much time, but when we are in a critical situation, that needs a quick response. I tell them so, and I try to let them know how important and risky the entire situation was at the start, without repeating it with every command. Then I let them know when that situation was over."*

"How do we assess the level of risk and importance of a situation or command? Is it my assessment of its risk on me or him?" asked Fahad as he petted Buraaq.

"That depends on how deeply you both understand each other, but the more transparent you are, the stronger your relationship will be. At the end, they are your brother and either of you might sacrifice himself for the safety of the other."

"And how do we reach such levels of trust with our totems?" asked Amer.

"That depends on your totem and its logic. Each totem builds trust and assesses it based on different criteria than other totems, but what I know for sure is that lying to your totem to make him follow your commands is the sure way to completely destroy that trust."

We spent the following few days training and practicing whenever the army stopped to camp. We did not have much time before my regiment would have to face an entire brigade without the support of the rest of this army.

185

Yasser Bahjatt ياسر بهجت

(13)

Ancient's Palace

Yasser Bahjatt ياسر بهجت

Saturday morning the twenty-seventh of Jumad the former 291 FG

We woke up early that morning, heading toward Granada. We took a path hidden between the forest trees and valley rocks. It was not the fastest route, but it was the most hidden and least used by the Spanish and their soldiers. Time flew by quickly as I explained to Sara and the craftsmen how the saed worked, how to build one, and how to prepare the poison silver and then mix it with salts and acids. The craftsmen were completely blown away by everything I told them about the saed, but I think I was blown much farther away by Sara. She had a sharp wit, was a fast learner and very observant, especially when we talked of tools and preparation It is rare that I find a female who cares for them, let alone to understand them this quickly.

When it was mid-day, the craftsmen excused themselves to return to the Narja and work on the build and preparations so that we could try out the saed the next day, when we returned from Granada. Additionally, they did not prefer to storm into Granada, as the risk of facing the soldiers of the Spanish throne was too high.

"Tell me about Al-Andalus."

She exhaled with sorrow and then spoke. "It is

189

said that it was the beacon to the world, and a center for productivity. It was a nation that harbored everyone. Its strength was in its acceptance. In fact, in its love for diversity, and its protection of its citizens' rights, regardless of their faith, race, or linage, it was able to gather civilizations from the corners of this earth, to mix them so that they became more beautiful."

"That is what we have heard from our ancestors, but this does not sound logical to me. How would a nation like that disappear?!"

"Human nature, greed, and vanity. Three hundred years after the liberation of Al-Andalus, internal struggles started between princes over the rule of Al-Andalus, causing them to become weak, but things did not stop there. In fact, enmity between them increased in search of power, to the point that they would not help their brethren when the Ferengi[1] attacked them. They would rather leave them to their dark fate, until they got to the point where they would fight their own brethren by the order of the Ferengi, or that one would kill his own father to rule."

"Three centuries before the struggle began?! Is history repeating itself?!"

"What do you mean?!"

"Never mind. Was there no wise man to unite them again?"

---

[1] Ferengi is the word Arabs used when referring to the White Man.

190

"How would one wise man stop a flood of fools?"

"What happened after the fall of Granada?"

"When Al-Zaghabi handed Granada to the Spanish, the treaty stated that the Spanish would allow everyone to keep their faith, no one would be forced out of his faith, their places of worship would remain intact, they would allow them to perform their ceremonies, and the Spanish would not confiscate their properties. In return, they would pay taxes to the Spanish throne."

"So why are you fighting them and hiding in caves? Isn't that contrary to the terms of the treaty?"

"What treaty? The Spanish did not uphold the treaty, but for a few short years. The start was against Christians from other denominations other than Catholic, especially Unitarians. After that, the inquisitions started to track down Jews, all while Muslims watched without even trying to help those they had sworn to protect from injustice when they liberated Al-Andalus a few centuries before that. We did not uphold our treaty with them when we left them with no protector. What we are doing now is an attempt at penance for what our fathers have done in servile. Enough talk of Al-Andalus. Tell me of Yaqteenya."

"It is a vast country that Allah had blessed with everything. Scattered across it are great cities from New Qurtuba in the east, to Al-Malayikeyah[1] in the

---

[1] Al-Malayikeyah (translation: The Angelic.

191

west, as far apart as Makkah and Akadeer. Between them are hills, mountain ranges, valleys, plains, forests, and deserts."

"New Qurtuba?! Al-Malayikeyah?! Those are your cities?"

"Two coastal cities. At the center of the first is a spacious square where all celebrations are held. None of its buildings is more than two stories high, and only minarets of its historical mosque and the tower of the old fortress cut through its horizon. As for Al-Malayikeyah, I have not visited since I was but a small boy. Its horizon is not that different from Qurtuba, aside from the mountains that surround it. Their buildings look very different from what I saw her. Qurtuba's buildings are covered with strange inscriptions and colors, for it is our custom that a child would celebrate his hundredth moon by being given paints and tools to draw whatever he wants on his house that remains unchanged until another child from the same house adds to it. While houses of Al-Malayikeyah are covered with different plants that their kids also plant when they are eighty moons old, both their harbors are simple and made for fishing boats. Rarely would you find one of the Yaqteenyan guard ships there."

"And how are its people? Do you all have the same faith?"

"Most of us are Muslims, yet some of us are still following the faiths of our ancestors without being *harassed to leave it, yet we still retain a lot of their heritage, especially our relationship with the rest of Allah's creation through our totems."*

"Your totems?"

"Each of us has a totem. It is his gateway to his relationship with the rest of Allah's creation." I then pointed at a huge vulture that was almost as large as Awqab, standing on one of the branches. Sara looked at him as he landed on my horse's back directly in front of me. She pulled out her weapon in panic.

"Do not be alarmed. He came upon my request." I extended my arm to pat him on the head and he moved nervously. "It seems that he is a bet frightened. He has not been used to humans talking to him."

"You are talking to him?"

"Yes, his name is Rapido. I asked him to accompany me for the rest of this mission."

"Do all Yaqteenyans talk to vultures?"

"Each of us discusses his totem. I am from the raptor totem. After we complete two hundred moons, we each start to learn about our totem from one of the masters at a Jamea[1] of those spread around all of Yaqteenya, where our scientists and masters from all fields of science gather to teach their disciplines to whomever wishes to learn ..."

She suddenly stopped and gestured to me to keep quite. We stood still for a few moments and I saw the palace walls above the mountain. She whispered into

---

[1] Jamea—Translation: From the word Jama, meaning to gather, so Jamea means the gatherer.

193

my ear, "Guards are everywhere. We will walk
without a sound until we reach one of the secret
entrances of Alhambra Palace. I have to blindfold you
now."

She pulled out her red napkin, and blindfolded
my eyes with it, at which point I asked Rapido to
soar around Alhambra Palace and keep a look out.

Some time had passed before we arrived to a
cave's entrance on the foothill of one of those hills. We
continued on our way, disappearing from Rapido's
sight, and we stopped after we went deeper into the
cave. "Get off of your horse. We will leave our horses
here."

I got off, and she took my hand to guide me
through the passageways of that cave, until we
reached stares that went upward, leading us to a
door. I felt the air sip through the door into the cave.
I think Sara and those around her were listening
carefully to make sure the area behind the door was
empty before they opened it. Sara refused to take off
my blindfold until we spent some time out of the cave
and went up another set of stairs. I was shocked to the
core in utter astonishment when she removed the
blindfold. We were in a hall with a dome decorating
roof in its center in a strange way that I have never
seen before. The last sun light of that day was
sneaking through the windows that had surrounded
the dome. Its walls were decorated with geometry and
verses of the Quran. In front of me was a window

194

that overlooked the palace's garden, where a pond of water stretched, surrounded by fountains from both sides.

"The Spanish had abandoned this place for centuries, but it was still standing, to remain a witness to what Al-Andalus once was. Sunset is but a few moments away. Hurry up if you want to capture some of the shadows of this place."

"I took out my saed and started to capture the shadows of everything my fights fell upon. Our companions were moving ahead of us to ensure that the place was empty before they allowed us to move. When I got out to the garden, I looked up to the sky, only to find Rapido was still soaring around the palace. I captured more shadows of the garden and its fountains and ponds.

"We need to leave immediately," I said to Sara.

"Why?"

"Pedro and his soldiers have arrived."

"How do you know that?"

"Rapido."

She looked sarcastically at me, then she pointed her scouts to check it out. They returned a few moments later, reporting that, "There is a large number of Spanish soldiers surrounding the place, ma'am, and a group of them led by Pedro himself is moving into the palace."

Her eyes widened with astonishment as she flipped her sight between me and the man. "How did Pedro know we were here?"

195

"I told him that I would meet the resistance here on this night."

"You led us here to be captured?" she asked, furiously, after she pulled out her dagger and placed it on my throat.

"I knew nothing of the resistance. I was only playing along so that he would bring me here to see the palace." She pushed her dagger, causing it to cut me and blood started dripping: "David was right. It was I who convinced him to trust you."

"I swear to you that I did not set this up, but I can help you get out of here." I slowly raised my hand to push the dagger away. "They are looking for me and they do not yet know that you are here. The majority of the soldiers are on the northern side of the palace. Their numbers are limited and far apart at the southern foothill. You can escape from the cave's entrance we came through, while I distract them here."

They looked at me with suspicion and hesitation. "Are we to leave you here so that you can tell them of our location?"

"You have blindfolded me whenever I was close to any of your secret locations. How am I to inform them? Run before they get to you."

She hesitated for a second before she signaled her companions to quietly retreat to their secret passage. Then she spoke. "We will wait for you in the forest, where I blindfolded you."

196

I marched toward the gate where Pedro would come in, stood crossing my arms in front of my chest awaiting him as the final sunlight vanished. He stopped suddenly after he crossed the gate and I came into the halo of his men's torches. I smiled cynically and then spoke. "Pedro, I did not know that you were my informant here. Had I known, I would have saved myself the hardship of this trek, and told you everything you needed to know when we met the first time."

"I do not recall Turkish spies having such a sense of humor. Tell me where your informant is and where you hid the gold that you stole and I promise you I will kill you without torturing you first."

"You and your men crawl back under the rock you crawled out from under, and I promise not to open hell's gate upon you."

He giggled loudly. "You? Open hell's gates? On me? You and what army?"

I stuck my hand into my bag to pick up one of the bottles. I then raised my left hand up high, lowering it rapidly as I pointed toward a spot on the ground in front of him, while I threw the bottle in a theatrical motion, as if I was a warlock from one of those plays I attended with my mother when I was a kid. The bottle exploded with flames that went up a few feet into the sky, blocking me from Pedro's sight, and by the time the flames receded to a fire on the ground, Rapido appeared to them, standing behind it between them and me. My sword was laying on the *ground covered in fire. I heard muttering sounds spreading amongst the soldiers.*

"You think that the soldiers of the Spanish throne would tremble in fear of a vulture?"

I raised my eyes to the sky, where vultures' sounds thundered, then the sky started raining vultures until hundreds of vultures gathered around me, and all of their eyes focused on Pedro as he reflected the fires of the ground and the soldiers' torches.

"You are all amongst the dead now. These vultures only gather to rip corpses."

I screamed once, and with it all the vultures took off toward Pedro and his soldiers, and the soldiers ran racing the wind to escape, while Pedro stormed toward me as he pulled his sword out of its sheath. "This magic of yours does not scare me. You are the corpse these vultures will eat," he said, as he jumped over the fire.

Rapido picked up my sword from its grip, as I stepped aside to avoid Pedro's attack; I extended my arm out by my side to catch my sword that Rapido had dropped toward me. Pedro swung his sword hard to his left, only to be met by my sword's edge with such violence that it almost detached it from my fist. Rapido landed on his head and gripped on to some hair locks. Pedro raised his sword and swung it above his head in an attempt to strike Rapido. I took advantage of that moment to strike his fist with the side of my sword. He screamed in pain and dropped his sword. I moved my sword's tip to his neck. By the time it reached it, it was struck by a metal bullet that threw it out of my hand. I continued my movement to strike his jaw with my left fist, rendering him unconscious. I looked toward the spot where the bullet came from I saw a ghost in a bright white cape escaping to hide within the darkness.

I picked up my sword and returned it to its sheath. I looked at Pedro's body. "It is your lucky day that I am in such a hurry, and that I do not kill an unarmed man."

And I ran out of the palace toward the forest.

Yasser Bahjatt ياسر بهجت

(14)

Rapture

ياسر بهجت Yasser Bahjatt

Before dawn of Saturday the eleventh of Safar 290 FG

This is the promised day; this is the day of confrontation. I still cannot believe that we are on the grounds for this battle. The events seem like an annoying dream that will soon pass. I calmed myself with the thought that the Khalifa and wise men of the clans would not allow this battle to start, that they will surely find an exit from this predicament, but I stand in the Khalifa's tent near the northern banks of the red river, where the clans' chieftains are discussing the strategy for this battle for the third time. I was distracted by my own thoughts before the army general's yelling voice snatched me out of it. "Baz, is your regiment capable of carrying out this mission?"

"Yes, Sir, but don't you find a single regiment of only ten soldiers a little under-staffed to take out an entire brigade of marksmen?!"

"We do not know for sure that they are there. Additionally, you are not just any regiment. You are the regiment of totems, and your ability to use your totems in battle makes you a force to be reckoned with in this battle. We also cannot spare more soldiers away from the real battlefield. That is why you will have to join the fight if it turns out I was wrong."

"But we are not that force that you talk of. They spent but a few months in my class, and have not yet mastered their abilities to communicate with their totems, as Baz and I have, and as you know, they did not even start mixing that with their fighting skill, except in the past few days during our trek from Al-Oyoon to here."

"In all cases we will not send more than one regiment, and your regiment is by far the best for this mission, or would you rather we send someone else?"

Our mission was to circle around a hill on the other side of the Red River, where it meets with the Witshata River. The hill had a thick forest on its southern side. The head army strategist believes that Jabal's army must place a group of marksmen atop of that hill, especially now that his army has been camping here waiting for us for the past two days. Our mission was to reach them at the start of the battle when the marksmen showed themselves to support the main army.

The regiment moved before dawn to cross the Red River before night raised its curtains. Layl flew, racing daylight to scout the hill and the adjacent forest without being noticed, while Salb remained in the river and held on to Sara swimming upriver. Layl returned to us when we arrived to the foothill and the sun's desk was in risen in the sky.

"As expected, there is a group of soldiers in the forest moving fast toward the hilltop. They are more than a hundred, and behind are three cannons, escorted by ten soldiers each," said Shihaab.

"We will not reach them in time if we follow them through the forest. We must split up. Amer, Tiryaq, Qabid, and Shihaab, you are with me. We shall climb until we reach them. The rest of you will track them down through the forest led by Fida."

"You do not think we can climb with you?" said Saab, angrily.

"It's our totems. They will not be able to climb, and without them, we lose most of our power. Come on. You heard your captain's orders. Let us run as fast as we can to get there before the climbers," he answered as he winked at me in a clear challenge and then ran toward the forest.

Saab mumbled a few words that I did not get as he shook his head in understanding before he followed Fida along with the rest of his group.

"Follow me quietly. Do not be reckless. I do not want any injuries or any sounds that might alert them to our approach."

We climbed the eastern foothill and got to the top in a few short moments. Shaheen stood on my head before passing over the edge of the hill to ensure that the place was clear. He saw the first of the marksmen as they came out from between the trees onto this open space on top of the hill. I whispered, "They have arrived. Hold still. If they see us now, from this distance, they will strike us down before we can get to them. Qabid, ask your brother to slither above us on the hill's edge, and warn us if anyone gets too close. I will ask Shaheen to come down, as he is easier to spot and Hasss is less conspicuous."

We dangled for a few more moments in our places, waiting as the marksmen marched toward the northern foothill, and stood in formation.

"The marksmen have arrived," whispered Qabid into my ear.

And just as I was about to give the order to climb up and attack, we heard yells and rumbles coming from the forest, followed by the echo of falling tree trunks, then an explosion. Fida had started his fun before we did. Then racket caused disorder in the marksmen lines as their attention changed to the forest, and raised their bows and snipers toward it in anticipation.

"Now", we pushed our bodies upward to attack the marksmen. They had no infantry to protect them. Hass was the first to strike the ankle of the nearest marksmen to him with his poisonous fangs before he raced the wind to wrap around Qabid's arm as he came out from behind the foothill to move with unnatural speed striking with his two swords left and right. Those who were not scratched by his swords were surely so by Hass's fang. Tiryaq swung his sword, tossing Hood on one of the marksmen while he continued his sword's motion to strike the chest of one of them. Hood fell on the neck of one and stung him, then fell to the ground, only to sting another's foot *before he climbed back to his brother's body and hung onto his sword again. In the meantime, Amer's body was dripping spiders of all species and color, most of which were highly poisonous and they started spreading across the stones underneath the marksmen; that was why he insisted on rubbing us all with a scented oil that he said he trained his spiders not to bite any creature reeking of that smell, while it aggressively attacked anyone else. Amer does not have the ability that Fida and I have of interacting with more than one totem at the same time; that means that he does not coordinate his attacks with anyone other than Shawk, who was standing on Amer's helmet. Amer swung his head like a mad man while fencing his opponents, whose terror was indescribable when they were surprised by a giant spider swirling around his helmet, dangling by his web that he had woven there. He would then let go of his web to fly toward their faces or chests to bite the victim and pump its poison into their veins, causing their bodies to spasm before he shot his web toward Amer to swirl around his head once again, even before their bodies hit the ground. As for Shihaab and I, we were perfectly synchronous with Layl, Awqab, and Shaheen, who were swarming around us like a storm of feathers, claws, and peaks. That storm moved with us wherever we did; distracting the marksmen's attention, with movements, strikes, and annoying wounds. The element of surprise was on our side in the first few minutes before the marksmen reorganized*

207

to attack us, but they were enough to take almost thirty of them out of the fight, most of them poisoned, unconscious, or severely wounded. Five of them were killed, despite the fact that I had made it clear to my regiment not to kill Yaqteenyan unless it was necessary, as they were all our brethren. But this was not the time to think of that. We were still in an unbalanced fight, with five men and six totems against approximately seventy, most of whom had raised their pistols or bows toward us, while few unsheathed their swords. I heard the hiss of the first arrow that landed into one's throat, and before any of his mates realized his injury or the source of that arrow, a flash lit the forest, followed by the sound of a cannon explosion and a cannonball that cut through the marksmen lines, adding a few dead and about twenty injured to our day's harvest. Fida, Fahad, and Saab appeared from between the trees along with their totems, and their yells and growls got louder as they ran toward us. The marksmen released their arrows toward them, buying us a few seconds to attack again before they had time to put another arrow in their bows. Fida and the others hid under their shields from the incoming arrows. To an observer, it would seem as if the arrows were reflected back toward their throwers, as three of them were stuck by arrows raining in on them from the forest. The fight was now much more balanced; we were now fighting twelve swordsmen, while the rest were raining Fida and his company with their arrows, preventing them from coming any closer. A few minutes later, they started falling one by one without anyone of us doing a thing. The poisons of the rest of Tiryaq's spiders had kicked in. The remaining soldiers dropped their weapons and placed their hands over their heads in terror and surrender.

I signaled my regiment to stop. "Tie them up." I inspected my regiment. We had survived, thank Allah, and we were able to take them down. Amer was severely injured in his right leg.

Fida yelled victoriously as he stepped toward us and asked Fahd and Saab to return to the Forest with their totems.

"Tiryaq, check Amer's wound, then take care of their wounded and poisoned."

"How about we turn their plan against them? I asked them to bring the cannon up here so that we can use it on their army."

"Fine, but keep it hidden from everyone's sight until we get our signal. Our orders were clear: to take out the enemy's ability to use this hill for marksmen, then await any further orders."

Fida and I stepped toward the northern foothill to take a look at the battlefield. We saw Jabal on his horse between the two armies and it seemed that he had just finished a speech or a threat before he returned to the back lines of his army. My father stepped forward on his horse between the lines and started his speech to Jabal's army. I remember his

209

words, as he kept repeating them to me all night:

"Dear Yaqteenyans, We have no need to fight you today, for we are all brethren. We did not come here today to keep the Moors' Khalifa on the throne, but we are here today to protect the justice and peace that we have all been blessed with since our ancestors accepted them. The Moors have never treated us with anything other than respect and honor. They did not force their religion upon us. Those of us who chose their faith did so of our own accord, and those who remained true to our ancestors' faith did so of their own accord, as well. They did not wage war on you for that, neither did they boycott you for it. The Moors never took advantage of their rule over us to take away the fruit of land, for even the Khalifa only owns the palace that our ancestors built and his trade that he survives on. I urge you, by the bond of brotherhood and our blood that flows through your veins, to turn away from this evil that you have for us and for everyone who had followed the faith of the Moors. He who turns back now shall not be harmed or prosecuted, and those who join us will not be questioned. As for those who insist on casting out the Moors away from us and despising anyone who follows their faith, thus destroying all that we have built together for the past three centuries, we shall not be held back our fury nor will we show any mercy for you."

My father returned to the army's front lines and

*voices rose from Jabal's army that then turned into
rumbles, and a few moments later, hundreds of
soldiers from his army came out toward the Khalifa's
army. None of them unsheathed their swords; they
were joining the Khalifa's army. The sky above them
turned black. Our army tried to warn them, but it
was too late, as Jabal's arrows fell upon them,
striking most of them down with severe wounds. I
heard angry shouts calling out Allah's great name
from the Khalifa's army, and with them marched the
front lines toward Jabal's army.*

*The two armies collided in an epic battle such as
this land has not seen in about two centuries. It was
an unbalanced battle; the Khalifa's army was more
than double Jabal's. We were standing on a hill
behind enemy lines; we could throw some pretty
painful blows to them from there, but the foothill
between us and them was not very steep, meaning
that they could easily get to us. No, it is best that we
wait so that they do not know that we have control
over the hill. We will only attack them if we get clear
commands to do so, or if we got found out.*

*We worked together to push the cannon to the
edge of the hill, as placing it there would allow us to
use it for our advantage the moment our orders
arrived. Shihaab pointed to the other side of the battle
field: "What is that?"*

*We raised our heads to see a cloud of rising dust
storming through the back lines of Jabal's army into
the heart of the battle. I raised my scope to see a horde*

of running bears and behind them were a few knights and footmen.

"Saab, have you ever seen anything like this before?"

I handed him my scope. "This is strange. Bears do not work in a horde. The horde is breaking through our lines without attacking anyone. Our soldiers were either moving out of its way in shock, or they pushed them out of the way, but to what end?!"

"They are heading for the Khalifa. It does not seem that anyone had noticed yet. We must warn them."

I do not recall who said that, but I replied, "I will send Awqab to warn them. I hope someone from the raptor totem is with them to understand him." Awqab flew off, gliding over the battlefield while changing direction and motion to avoid getting hit by arrows or bullets.

"What if they could not understand him? Or if someone struck down Awqab? No, we must warn them; we must protect the Khalifa, no matter the cost." By the time Fida had finished his sentence, he was on Hakoom's back and Heraak had stormed out in front of him.

I yelled, "Fida! Wait! We are behind enemy lines! You will not get to him! This is suicide!"

But he ignored me, as he moved away as fast as an arrow.

"We must follow him," yelled Fahad, as he ran

downhill behind him.

"I will send Naab with you while I remain here, where I can provide cover with my sniper and bow. Amer can operate the cannon to cause chaos around you."

I looked into the eyes of the rest of my regiment. I saw their determination to follow Fida and protect the Khalifa.

"Very well. Stay together. Our mere act of going down this foothill will be enough for our enemy to know that his marksmen are down to the Khalifa."

Fida had already gone half way downhill, and was approaching the river fast. It seemed that the enemy had not yet noticed Fida or did not pay him much attention, but the moment we started descending from that foothill, I saw a decent number of soldiers change direction toward their back lines and the river, where Salb was waiting with Sara. Heraak passed in front of Salb as he crossed the river in speed and Fida in pursuit. I heard Salb speaking to Fida, but Fida did not pay much attention to him. By the time Heraak got out of the river's water, the first warriors had reached him, then rammed him, throwing him aside as he continued his path, striking left and right with his horns, opening a path for Hakoom. Salb retreated into the river to get closer to us and farther from the attackers. Loads of warriors entered the river to attack Salb and face us when we got there. When they got mid-way into the river, Salb dived under its waters, while Fahad and Buraaq

213

stood on its shoreline, waiting for the rest of us. I got to the river and pushed through it and my regiment followed me. Seconds later, we heard soldiers' screams that were interrupted because they were choking on the river water, as if something was dragging them down. Then their bodies would pop up as they floated downstream surrounded by the red hue of their blood. That must have been Salb and Sara's doing. I met my first soldier and stabbed him in his throat with my sword as I struggled through the river's water to get passed him. The rest of my regiment arrived to face the soldiers. A bloody battle had started in this river that had changed its water's color, making it a truly red river. Badr's arrows and bullets were bringing down soldiers around us, while cannonballs were sometimes mowing down the flux of soldiers coming toward us and others clearing the way for Fida. Shaheen was flying above me, giving me details of the battle around me, and warning me of soldiers' movements that I might not notice, but he was unable to join this fight; the water would obstruct his ability to fly and maneuver. As for Layl, he had to return to the forest, for owls are not used to staying awake until this time of day, Tiryaq threw a hood over the river to thin down the soldiers' numbers that cross over to us. We only had four totems left with us; all of them moved well in this river's waters, but Sara, without a doubt, was the master of this battle. We still could not cross this river. We were seven men and *four totems facing an endless flow of warriors. Whenever we killed one of them, three others took his place. It was a lost cause; the outcome of this battle was clear, but we refused to surrender. We must catch up to Fida; we must protect the Khalifa. Shaheen gave me a warning and I shouted, "Fahad!" Fahad looked at me, and I saw his eyes pop out as the life drew out of them after an arrow struck his head and the river dragged him away. I swung my sword with anger, chopping off my opponent's arm and following it with a punch from my left fist to his head, making him slip into the red river's water. He held on to my leg to pull me down with him, but I kicked him in the face a few times before he let go of me and I struggled to get back above the water. As I tried to regain sight of what was going on around me, an assailant threw a stab at me. I could not block it, but his sword was planted into Naab's body, who had intercepted it to save me. I raised my left arm to plant my dagger in his jaw. I then twisted it before I pushed his corpse away from me. I saw Buraaq battling the river with an amputated arm. The world went dark. I had failed my regiment. How did I allow this to happen! I must get my regiment out of this slaughter house. I do not recall much after that; I was fighting like a mad man. I do not recall how many we killed, nor who of my regiment was still alive, but I got back to reality by Saab's voice. "Baz, ride on Fazza's back and hold on tight."*

I complied without thinking, I did not know what

215

he was planning, or maybe I did, but opted to save myself. Was I a coward then?! Did I leave my regiment to die so that I could save my own skin?! I do not know, but Fazza pushed forward with such power, getting me out of the river to catch up with Fida. I looked behind and saw that Saab had an arrow sticking out of his left side while he swung his lance in every direction, causing death all around him. I saw a soldier being pulled into the depths of the river. I knew that Salb and Sarab were still alive, but for how long? A group of soldiers blocked my sight as they tried to catch me. I could no longer see the river.

Now was not the time to cry, but I could not help myself. I was crying like a baby in his mother's arms. I screamed with all the air I still had in my chest. Why? Why all of this blood? I was dripping of water and blood—mine, my regiment's, Yaqteenyan blood, Moorish blood, totem blood. No difference. They were all red. Where did we find the difference that made us spill it all? No time to cry now. I must get back to the fight. Fazza was sticking anyone who got in his way with his claws until I saw Hakoom's horns. I was near Fida, I looked ahead and found that the bears' horde had already broken through the Khalifa's perimeter, and that a group of Jabal's knights had reached it and struck down most of the Khalifa's guards. I almost reached Fida when Hakoom stopped and pushed his body forward with his two back legs, *tossing Fida into the air. Fida tossed his shield before he landed on the ground to cut off a pullet from a short-range pistol that was flying toward the Khalifa. Fazza swayed, and his arms lost their grip on the ground, forcing his body to slide a few feet forward before I fell off of his back. He had been hit by several arrows and bullets, yet he stood back up on his two legs, attacking the soldiers around him with his claws. I raised my sword to block an axe's strike, while stabbing its carrier in the thigh with my dagger, then followed it by planting my sword in his chest. I stood to find myself in the midst of the Khalifa's guard, of whom only a handful remained. I looked behind me and saw my father and the Khalifa fencing side by side. Shaheen and Awqab came down to join me, and we fought valiantly. I saw an arrow flying toward my father. I ordered Shaheen to spread his wings and fly like the wind to catch the arrow with his small body, forcing it to change direction away from my father. I saw a speed hit Fazza in the chest and his body collapsed with one last roar as it was filled with arrows and sword slashes. A few soldiers still stood between us and the Khalifa, and only my father and the bearer of the red flag that had the words "Allah Akabr,"[1] who was fighting with his other hand. I saw a spear flying toward the Khalifa, but it hit the flag bearer in the chest. The Khalifa caught the flag before it fell out of the man's hand. Fida was fighting like a*

---

[1] Allah Akbar—Translation: God is greater.

raging bull, trying to break through the lines to reach the Khalifa. I never knew that the Khalifa was such a skilled warrior. He was using his sword and the flag's lance all at once, without ever dipping the flag for even a second. He was so keen on keeping it high. Fida reached the Khalifa and their eyes met, and I saw content in his eyes that suddenly turned into concern. He stepped forward toward Fida, and embraced him before he spun around himself and a sword that was meant for Fida, who went through his body. He collapsed as he handed the flag to Fida and shouted, "Allah Akbar is not to be dipped," before he fell into a pond of his blood, and then a shout echoed: "We killed the Khalifa, we killed the Khalifa." And with that shout, the enemy's soldiers started their retreat from around the Khalifa, and with that, retreated the last sunlight of that day. I heard Fida's screams as he struck with his sword and flag lance in every direction, striking down the retreating soldiers around him before someone stabbed him in his chest. The stab did not go all the way through, as a man in a flaming red cape appeared to grab the stabber's hand and twist it, shattering it with a frightening sound before he could push the sword all the way in, only to disappear among the crowds without a trace. I ran toward Fida, who leaned on the flag's lance and looked at me with pale eyes. "The Khalifa is dead. My father is dead." He then fell unconscious.

◦❖❖❖❖❖❖❖◦

I was waiting, worried, in front of the Khalifa's tent. My father was inside with the healer as he examined Fida. Time passed slowly for me, not knowing how Fida was. He was bleeding badly when they carried him there. The healer did not seem optimistic when he ordered everyone out. The healer came out and my father was right behind him.

"How is he, Healer?"

"It is a miracle. The sword's tip stopped exactly on his heart. If it had advanced the length of even one more finger, he would have died, no doubt. An infection has started around the wound and his condition is unstable, but he is alive for now."

"Go to him. He has asked for you," my father said to me in a soft, caring voice.

I entered the tent, and stood next to his bed as my eyes filled with tears and my father stood right behind me. I found him writing on a sheet with a broken arrow. He raised his eyes for our eyes to meet, and feelings of sadness and grief flowed between us.

"Any news of the totem regiment?"

"We did not receive anything about them yet. Fighting has not stopped at the marksmen hill yet."

"Do you remember our talk in the forest?" I nodded in the affirmative. Then he continued. "We must stop this strife. We must protect the blood of Yaqteenya. Revenge was the first thought that passed

219

through my head when I saw the death of my father, but I know now that I must stop this war to honor his memory. I need you, Baz, to cross the Okeanós and return to us with the truth and its evidence, whatever that truth may be, and let the Yaqteenyans make whatever decision they want to then."

Fida's body shuddered, his eyelids shivered while his eyeballs rolled in the back of his head, and the sheet fell from his hands.

I called out, "Healer!"

The healer entered the tent and moved toward Fida's body, which lay lifeless. "All of you go out and bring me my assistant immediately."

I quickly picked up the sheet before my father pushed me outside and sent for the healer's assistant.

"I will not allow you to go."

"But it is the command of the Khalifa. He commanded with his last breath that I go."

"So have I promised my Khalifa to protect Yaqteenya and make sure no one crosses this Okeanós, and it is up to me now."

"I will go and no one will stop me."

"Guards, hold this man in a cell until the Khalifa decides what to do with him."

I never imagined that my father would throw me into a cell this quickly without discussion. I did not wish to resist the guards; Yaqteenya was wounded enough for one day. The guard led me to a wagon with iron bars that I entered in despair.

يقطينيا Yaqteenya

I sat in the corner of my prison cell. I took out the paper from my pocket to read it in the torch's flickering light. I found a poem that was etched into my memory, as Fida had etched it with his blood.

Centuries pass and you remain in our vision
                              How did we lose you when you were
                                            to the world a beacon?

We cry at your parting every day as if we were
                              There the day your destruction occurred

A year, nine decades, and two centuries, we've been apart
                              Shall we someday return to that habitat?

We stroll your palaces, what is left of our glory
                              We prospered the land with peace and justice,
                                            and to the world we were exemplary

I pity our state, what had our people done to you
                              We carry your morals as would an animal's
                                                          zoo

We sing of love that we hide in our hearts
                              We lie, does a lover cause his loved one such
                                                          destruction

Allah's religion that revered you we
abandoned

> And we roam the land with denial and
> defilement

It is a thought echoed in my head I would not
utter

> Had we left you, or was it you who tired of
> dishonor

For we in sleep and ignorance have
disappointed

> Everyone who had torrentially justice had
> spread

We say the flow of justice by west was
tightened

> Yet we fight each other and steal spans of land

Oh, Andalus, I swear you had caused us no
injustice

> What wiped us out of your land was our
> injustice

Awaken nation of Islam, how many have we
> Of Andalus that is defiled by what we for ages
> did carry

Is it not enough to remind us as a calamity?
Is it not enough the damage this humiliation
has brought upon thee

Awaken and stand strong to support our
people
For we want not for Andalus to repeat

Establish as our lord has asked justice
For anything else we want no insistence

For when you return to a religion that has
made us proud
Only then will Al-Andalus call comeback
aloud

I did not understand at the time, but I know now that he knew what had happened in Al-Andalus, and that his fear of us following in their footsteps was weighing heavily on him—the fear of history repeating itself, and that we would cause our own destruction.

Yasser Bahjatt ياسر بهجت

(15)
Al–Monqad

These pages were written in Spanish, so I translated them into Arabic. It seems that they were written in the same memoir, after the pages that Al-Baz wrote.

Night of Tuesday the first of Jumad the latter 291 FG

I am not used to using the fall of Granada as a historical reference, but after reading what Al-Baz wrote in his memoirs, I have decided to maintain the same calendar. It is much closer to my heart, so that we would not forget that day.

We arrived at Jabal Tariq a few hours after sunset following a couple of days' travel from Narja. Al-Baz has delivered on his promises to us. We are able to build the shadows hunter and the echo knitter after a group of us were able to get the clock maker out of Granada while the Spanish soldiers were busy fighting Al-Baz. I still do not believe that Al-Baz has the ability to communicate with raptors, or his claim of defeating the Spanish soldiers with the support of a flock of vultures. What was even stranger was that when he found me in the forest that night, he was accompanied by an owl named Hinchado, which he said helped him find me, despite the darkness of that night, along with the vulture he named Rapido, which he recruited that morning in the forest. They are both now with us and Al-Baz is using the owl to help us scout the area.

"Cannons are scattered around the mountain on moonless nights more than others. As on such nights, the Turks deliberately sail near the Jabal Tariq, but

227

on the edge of the Spanish cannons' range, while the Spanish try to sink their ships. It is a political war game they have been playing for more than a century, and the Spanish, in all of this time, were never able to sink a single Turkish ship. Astonishingly, the Spanish cannonballs had nicked the sides of Turkish ships many times," I said, explaining the reason so many soldiers were deployed on the coastline, whose torches we could clearly see on this moonless night.

"And why do the Turks get so close to the Spanish?"

"I think they deliberately intimidate them to show them that they do not fear them and that they knew their cannons' exact capabilities and locations."

"So how will I reach Sibtah before Al-Anqaa leaves?"

"The Spanish anchor some small boats on the outer edges of the complex. We will steal one and sail in the darkness of the night without being noticed, but I do not promise that we can catch Al-Anqaa before she sails, and you cannot get close to her, let alone sneak on board if we tried to get to her at sea."

Al-Baz nodded in understanding, and signaled Hinchado to fly into the night. He returned a few moments later and stood on Al-Baz's shoulder.

"He says there is a boat a thousand feet or so away in this direction, guarded by only two guards."

I signaled my companions to move forward in the

direction that Al-Baz had pointed. Al-Baz followed them and I was on his tail. We easily disposed of the two guards, as our emergence from the night's darkness took them off guard for a second, which was all we needed.

"You must hide quickly. A group of soldiers is coming our way," whispered Al-Baz.

We hid behind a bunch of boxes scattered around us, and then we heard the soldiers approaching. They stopped at the boat.

"Where are Denial and Paolo?" asked the group's captain.

"I do not know, Sir. They are supposed to be here awaiting orders."

"When I find them, they will be punished for leaving their posts without prior approval. This is not their first offense. Get a move on. Unload this boat. We must get this ammunition to the top of the mountain before midnight."

I whispered into Al-Baz's ear. "There were never cannons atop Jabal Tariq's peak before. Raising such huge cannons to the mountain's peak is a daunting task. They must know that Al-Anqaa will pass here tonight, and this will be their attempt to sink the Ottoman navy's crown ship."

"We must get rid of them, then."

"Why would you want to help them when you know they will arrest you if they find you?"

"How can I watch and do nothing, allowing a Muslim to be killed? Is that not what destroyed Al-

229

Andalus?! How can you change history if you repeat the same mistakes of those who came before you?"

I exhaled in frustration, but he was right. We must try and stop the Spanish from sinking the Ottoman's strength symbol, even if they were indifferent to our predicament, and never offered us any real assistance, for they are first and foremost our brothers in faith.

"We need to know the soldiers' and cannons' deployment on the mountain. Would you ask Hinchado to check it out?"

"I see you finally believe that I spoke to birds?"

"No, but there is no harm in entertaining ourselves in such situations to reduce our fear and anxiety."

Al-Baz smiled as he released the owl. I pointed my men to move toward the mountain, guided only by what little light reached us from the Spanish soldiers' torches that had dimmed on their way to us. If we lit any lantern or torch, we would announce our presence and that would be our doom. We did not face any soldiers, as most of them were gathered around the cannons, awaiting their orders to start the bombardment. When we arrived to the edge of the mountain, we heard a trumpet that echoed all around us, and with it, all torches and scattered lanterns were put out, and darkness moved in, safe from the twinkles of stars in the sky. I stood still, for how were we to climb the mountain without seeing where we set our feet! I heard flapping wings approach and then they vanished next to me; it must be the owl returning to Al-Baz. I whispered, "We cannot make any move in this darkness. Let's return to the boat and get out of here."

"True. You will not be able to make a move. As for me, I will move with Hinchado."

I held his arm. "What madness! One of the soldiers might hear your footsteps, or you might bump into them, or even fall off a cliff without knowing."

"I told you, Hinchado will guide me, and no one will hear my footsteps. I am good at sneaking around, as you know. Please hold this for me. If I do not return, please take my notes to Fida in New Qurtuba behind the Okeanós and show him my ring as evidence that I gave it to you." He then put this notebook in my hand and his ring around my finger. I tried to hold him again, but my hands found nothing but emptiness. I whispered his name a few times, but he did not answer. He had vanished into the night. Lord protect him and return him safely to me.

◆❖❖❖❖❖❖❖◆

Time went by so slowly as we waited at the boat on the east side of Jabal Tariq. I do not know how much time had passed, minutes or hours. If I were not certain that days would not pass without a sunrise, I

231

would have though it to be days. Then a shiver went through my body as I heard an explosion near Jabal Tariq and with it, a flash lit up the night. The Spanish had fired their first cannon, and with that flash, shadows appeared in the sea that seemed to be a ship's ghost.

Successive explosions and flashes lit up the coast around Jabal Tariq. I picked up my scope and pointed it toward the ship. It was coming closer with every explosion. It was madness that pushed those warriors to challenge each other so openly. I raised my scope toward Jabal Tariq in hopes of finding some sign of Al-Baz, but the foothill had blocked the lights from the cannons and torches from lighting what was atop the mountain. I saw no sign of Al-Baz or any cannons there. Did the Spanish soldiers trick us to lure us to the mountain? But how did they know that we were listening then? Or was Al-Baz successful in getting rid of them? I wish I could find an answer. My heart was beating in fear of losing him. How did this happen? How do I feel this way toward a stranger whom I only met but a few days ago? These are normal feelings of anxiety. No, no, they are not. I had sent many men on missions before, but I never felt this anxious.

I swept the mountain top again with my scope, in hopes of find anything that would calm me down. There, on the peak, a dim spark; yes, there it was again. I started seeing a light growing at the

mountain top until it became a raging fire in but a
few seconds, and a huge explosion erupted, throwing
debris in every direction. Huge cannons fell off the
mountain's cliff. Some fell into the sea, others on top
of the soldiers on the beach. A cloud of smoke rose
from the mountain top, lit by the raging fire of the
explosion. A few shadows appeared behind the smoke.
It looked like a few men had gathered to face a single
man. It must have been Al-Baz. Shadows of wings
circling the area reflected off the smoke. They must
have been the owl and vulture that accompanied him.
The shadows entangled and mixed. I could almost
hear the clanks of swords colliding; the smoke slowly
faded away. I could see Al-Baz clearly now, as he
fenced a soldier and Pedro, while the vulture and owl
circled Al-Baz and moved with him as if they were an
extension of him. Pedro pointed toward the remaining
cannon. Al-Baz tried to reach the cannon, but Pedro
and the soldier kept cutting him off, while the other
soldiers worked on loading and aiming it. Al-Baz
escaped Pedro's blockade and jumped toward the
cannon's nozzle, causing it to change direction at the
same moment a cannonball rushed out of it toward
Al-Anqaa.

I moved my scope toward Al-Anqaa, where the
waters directly behind it had exploded, but it was not
hit. I returned my scope toward Al-Baz. He must
escape now. He had successfully completed his
mission. Oh, lord, he was hanging onto the cannon's
nozzle, dangling over the mountain's edge. Pedro

stormed toward the cannon in clear anger, and started kicking the cannon. He was trying to push the cannon over and Al-Baz along with it. The vulture held onto Al-Baz as he flapped his wings frantically in an attempt to help Al-Baz, then the cannon slipped off the mountain's cliff. I will never forget the look on Al-Baz's face at that moment. There was neither terror nor fear, but confidence and happiness. Seconds later, I heard the sound of the cannon colliding with the rocks. I screamed bitterly, "No, Baz! No!"

The world went dark to me after that. I did not feel my men as they dragged me and returned me to Narja. I tried to find out what had happened to Al-Baz after that, but my men could not get to the point where the cannon had fallen to try and find his corpse. Nothing remained to keep his memory alive other than this notebook that was his most valuable possession.

سارة

بهاء الدين

بني غامق

لون العين
(رمادي)

فاتح البشرة

عالِم

بلاد الكنانه

القاهره
الجديده

الملائكه
عابدين جبل
أوشانا الدخان قرطبه
العيون الصغيره
أباستلو الحسيني ابن عبدالله

بغداد
الجديده

السفحاء

جاور السحاب

45179612R00143

Printed in Poland
by Amazon Fulfillment
Poland Sp. z o.o., Wrocław